His eyes watched her closely

"Don't be deceived by Thailand's surface, Lousiana. Behind the facade, paradise awaits."

Her eyes locked with his. "I didn't come in search of paradise, Gunner."

His voice was low and seductive. "Maybe you could use a little."

Some long-hidden desire snaked just beneath her skin, but she briskly rubbed her hands along her arms in an attempt to make the sensation go away. "I came here to find my brother. You know something about his disappearance, Gunner. You know that he's in some kind of danger, don't you?"

Gunner stared into that incredibly soft but determined face and felt himself sliding into a trap of his own making. The woman spelled trouble, but he didn't know what he was going to do about her.

"This is not a corporate boardroom, Louisiana. Civilized rules simply don't apply."

"I'm not afraid."

"You should be."

ABOUT THE AUTHOR

A native of Oklahoma, Andrea Davidson graduated from the University of Missouri and began her writing career with the American Medical Association in Chicago. She free-lanced for medical journals and magazines after the birth of her children, then turned to romance writing. Andrea now lives in Texas with her family.

Books by Andrea Davidson

HARLEQUIN INTRIGUE
25—A SIREN'S LURE
41—OUT FROM THE SHADOWS

HARLEQUIN AMERICAN ROMANCE
122—AN UNEXPECTED GIFT
324—THE BEST GIFT OF ALL
371—THE LIGHT ON WILLOW LANE

Tiger's Den

Andrea Davidson

Harlequin Books

TORONTO • NEW YORK • LONDON
AMSTERDAM • PARIS • SYDNEY • HAMBURG
STOCKHOLM • ATHENS • TOKYO • MILAN
MADRID • WARSAW • BUDAPEST • AUCKLAND

In memory of Jim, for a lifetime of adventure.
Thanks to Andi for her creative spark.

Harlequin Intrigue edition published November 1992

ISBN 0-373-22203-3

TIGER'S DEN

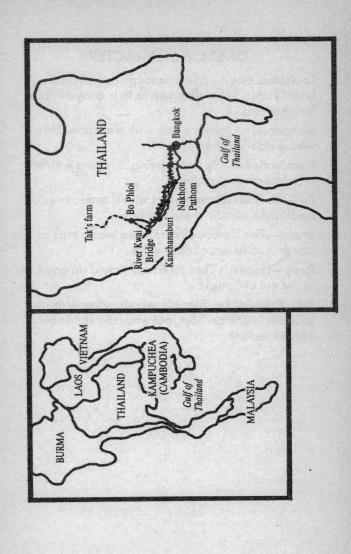

THAILAND

Bangkok

Gulf of
Thailand

Tak's farm

Bo Phloi

River Kwai
Bridge

Kanchanaburi

Nakhon
Pathom

BURMA

LAOS

VIETNAM

THAILAND

KAMPUCHEA
(CAMBODIA)

Gulf of
Thailand

MALAYSIA

CAST OF CHARACTERS

Louisiana Bond—She was tough as nails in the boardroom, but walking on nails in a mysterious foreign land.

Gunner—The mystery man with a mission. But whose side was he on?

Hamlin Bond—He was missing . . . along with a priceless ancient statue.

Po—The Buddhist monk lost with Hamlin; even meditation couldn't help him now.

Bruno—This Cambodian refugee was a man of few words . . . and lots of dirty work.

Roxy—Hamlin's Thai girlfriend would do anything to get out of Bangkok.

Mrs. Kruger—Louisiana's secretary knew the oil business inside and out, but what did she know about Hamlin?

Kubla Khan

In Xanadu did Kubla Khan
A stately pleasure-dome decree:
Where Alph, the sacred river, ran
Through caverns measureless to man
  Down to a sunless sea.
So twice five miles of fertile ground
With walls and towers were girdled round:
And there were gardens bright with sinuous rills,
Where blossomed many an incense-bearing tree;
And here were forests ancient as the hills,
Enfolding sunny spots of greenery.

But oh! that deep romantic chasm which slanted
Down the green hill athwart a cedarn cover!
A savage place! as holy and enchanted
As e'er beneath a waning moon was haunted
By woman wailing for her demon-lover!
And from this chasm, with ceaseless turmoil seething,
As if this earth in fast thick pants were breathing,
A mighty fountain momently was forced:
Amid whose swift half-intermitted burst
Huge fragments vaulted like rebounding hail,
Or chaffy grain beneath the thresher's flail:
And 'mid these dancing rocks at once and ever
It flung up momently the sacred river.
Five miles meandering with a mazy motion
Through wood and dale the sacred river ran,
Then reached the caverns measureless to man,
And sank in tumult to a lifeless ocean:
And 'mid this tumult Kubla heard from far
Ancestral voices prophesying war!

  The shadow of the dome of pleasure
  Floated midway on the waves;

Where was heard the mingled measure
From the fountain and caves.

It was a miracle of rare device,
A sunny pleasure dome with caves of ice!

A damsel with a dulcimer
In a vision once I saw:
It was an Abyssinian maid,
And on her dulcimer she played,
Singing of Mount Abora.
Could I revive within me
Her symphony and song,
To such a deep delight 'twould win me,

That with music loud and long,
I would build that dome in air,
That sunny dome! those caves of ice!
And all who heard should see them there,
And all should cry, Beware! Beware!
His flashing eyes, his floating hair!
Weave a circle round him thrice,
And close your eyes with holy dread,
For he on honey-dew hath fed,
And drunk the milk of Paradise.

—Samuel Taylor Coleridge

Where Alph, the sacred river, ran
Through caverns measureless to man
Down to a sunless sea.

The Legend

For two thousand years it lay shrouded in the mists of time. There had been a king and a faith. There had been treasures beyond mortal imagination. Even beyond, some said, that of the gods themselves.

Before the Mongols came and sacked, temples and monasteries were built to the Enlightened One. The foundations were laid beside the sacred rivers and those great ancestral voices prophesied a civilization to rival all others. Amid the splendor, saffron-draped novices and monks and high priests, their heads shorn smooth and brown, sought liberation from the endless cycle of birth and death and suffering.

And a jade Buddha sat in stony silence and watched it all.

But like wind against shale, the years wore steadily away. Fires raged, floods saturated, wars ravaged. The great warriors from the east closed in.

A silent monk, emaciated and seeking transcendence, painstakingly carved secrets on the back of the jade statue, telling in pictures and cryptic letters a story of priests who, in the dark of the night, stealthily carried the king's treasures piece by piece into the high caves where weather and looters and Mongols could not defile them. The civilization fell to ruin and others followed. The wheel of life turned endlessly. Around and around.

Lost in the tangled jungle, beneath a mask of steam, the jade Buddha lay on the moist valley floor, sundered from its ancient altar and place of veneration. Waiting.

Waiting for a thousand years for its secret to be revealed.

And 'mid this tumult Kubla heard from far
Ancestral voices prophesying war!

Chapter One

Louisiana Bond sat in Billy Boone Bond's walnut-paneled office, with its smell of cigar tobacco permanently embedded in the rich brown carpet and expensive upholstered furniture. The thick leather chair creaked as she swung toward the six-line phone that was ringing on his desk.

It was *her* desk, actually. And her office now that her father was dead. But even though Billy Boone had buried himself, his Lear jet and his twenty-five-year-old bride-to-be in the middle of the Gulf of Mexico more than four years ago, she still thought of the office as his.

It held his smells, his colors, his indelible style. There were pictures on the wall of Billy Boone with every president since Ike. There were framed clippings from the *New York Times* and the *Wall Street Journal* on that day back in '52 when he bought out Yeager Oil and joined the ranks of the ten wealthiest men in the country. The shelves in the large office were lined with his invaluable collections of Western bronzes. The six-line phone on the desk had been installed by him.

Beyond the window, the four thousand some acres of Texas sagebrush and mesquite that served as a backyard had been purchased back in '61 by him—along, of course, with the twenty thousand acres next door that housed his cattle and oil wells.

Even Mrs. Kruger, the heavily starched German who had immigrated with her parents to Fredericksburg back in 1934, and who was now sitting in the adjacent office, had been his secretary before becoming hers. After his death, Mrs. Kruger had chosen to stay on. After working for someone as excessive and colorful as Billy Boone Bond, moving to an ordinary office job would have been equivalent to a slow form of dry rot.

The only thing Louisiana had added to the office was a computer—a monstrous thing that Daddy Bond would have labeled "god-awful," but would, in his homespun, practical way, have come to appreciate as a useful and necessary evil in the high-stakes scramble for power, prestige and the almighty dollar.

"Well, spit across the county line," Louisiana said to the man at the other end of the phone line. "Now, Jake, you know I don't have time for any old nuisance suit. Why don't you just tell that old buzzard that he's got about as much chance as a fly on flypaper to get me into court on negligence. He was the one who hired the incompetent boob who fell off the rig, not me. Maybe you should remind him that Billy Boone set the standard for safety precautions on these drilling operations and I've maintained that same... Oh, hell's bells, Jake, hang on. Another one of these damn lines is ringing."

Louisiana punched the hold button and stabbed the blinking light. "The lease agreement is right here on the screen now, Sid," she said to the caller. "No, no, I'm going after mineral rights only. Why don't we just sit on it for a few days and let her think about it. She's just a sweet little old lady, sugar, and I'm not about to kick her out of house and home. Life estate is a possibility, but if she doesn't want that, then I'm only going after the minerals. Now don't rush me, Sid honey," she added sweetly. "I'll wrangle the best deal for us. After all, don't I always?"

Mrs. Kruger came into the office with a heavy stack of mail just as Louisiana jabbed the other button and resumed the previous conversation. "Listen, Jake honey, I'd just love to jaw some more about this negligence thing, but I've really got to go. I've got more butter on my bread right now than I can spread. And I just know you'll be able to clean up this little mess. If you want to you can tell him that his boy falling cost me three days' drilling time, and if he continues to pester me with this ridiculous lawsuit, I'm going to throw a lynching party and *he's* going to be the guest of honor."

Louisiana hung up the phone without saying goodbye. But then she never said goodbye. Never said hello, either. She had inherited that habit from Daddy Bond, who claimed such niceties were a waste of time. "If you're talkin'," he'd say, "then they're gonna know you're there, right? And if you ain't and the line goes dead, then any dimwit should be able to figure out that you've hung up." Billy Boone Bond never won any awards for congeniality. But congeniality didn't make you one of the ten wealthiest men in the country, either.

Louisiana flicked her hand over the six-line telephone. "I hate this thing," she said to Mrs. Kruger. "All it does is ring."

Mrs. Kruger sorted the mail into precise stacks on the desk. "You would like me to have it removed?"

"Gracious sakes alive, no! Daddy would roll over in his grave. Is that my magazine?"

Mrs. Kruger hesitated for one split second as if she wasn't going to hand it over. Finally, and with great reluctance, she did, but not without shaking her head and clucking. "I do not understand how it is that you can read such trash, Miss Bond. The men in that thing are so, so—"

Louisiana couldn't hide the grin. "Why, Mrs. Kruger, have you taken to reading *Adventures in Warfare,* too? I'm shocked. I really am."

"I—I most certainly have not," she stammered in outrage, then turned and, with an economy of brisk little steps, left the office, closing the door soundly behind her.

Louisiana chuckled and sat back in the big leather chair, propping her red lizard-skin boots up on top of the desk. As an afterthought, she leaned forward and disarmed the phone. For one brief second she anticipated getting caught, as if Billy Boone Bond himself might walk in and find her neglecting her duty as his rightful heir. It was a responsibility she never took lightly, but she wondered sometimes if the price she had to pay was worth it. She hadn't asked for the job as chairman of Bond Enterprises. It had been dumped in her lap. Her daddy had simply said one day, "Darlin', this here is yours and your brother's as much as mine, and since that boy's about as useful to the business as a stripped bolt, you're gonna have to do it all someday. I suggest you ready yourself."

She hadn't been ready and, even after four years, she knew there were those in the company fold who thought of her as nothing more than a tin-quarter counterfeit, a little girl playing big-boy office. *Nobody could ever fill Billy Boone Bond's shoes,* they said. *Give up the act!* they cried. Sometimes Louisiana thought they were right. While she *was* his rightful heir, it often felt like a charade. And in some secret place deep inside of her, she occasionally wondered if she even wanted to play.

Pushing the momentary doubts away, she concentrated solely on the magazine in her lap. She bypassed the Vietnam recaps, but paused now and then over photographs of rugged-looking mercenaries in camouflage—an impulsive and somewhat futile thing to do, but aesthetically pleasing nonetheless. She flipped through advertisements for every kind of lethal weapon known to man until she reached the classifieds.

"Explosives made easily, cheaply, from farm fertilizer, blast dugouts, trenches, rocks. Instructions $3." Nope, that wasn't what she was looking for.

Some people probably read the magazine for its articles, others to fulfill a latent adventurous need. Louisiana read it for the classifieds.

There would be a message in here for her somewhere. There was one for her every week.

"The Wolf is taking on new contracts. Will consider all situations. P.O. Box 2665, Joplin, MO." *Very subtle,* she thought, rolling her eyes and moving on to the next one.

Adventures in Warfare was a soldier-of-fortune weekly, published out of Bangkok, Thailand, by her half brother, Ham Bond. Ham was older by six years, and if their family situation had been a normal one, the years between them might have been too wide to form a close relationship. As it was, most people said the Bond family situation bordered on odd.

Billy Boone Bond had been what the press liked to call "a ladies' man." Louisiana wasn't sure about the lady part of it, but she did know that her daddy had formed the habit of falling for every pretty young thing he met and, perhaps because he had been the son of a Southern Baptist preacher, he had felt obligated to make honest women out of each and every one of them. The trouble was, the marriages never lasted. The women Billy Boone chose to marry just didn't have an image of hearth and home at the center of their being. As Billy liked to say, "They were restless as hens on a hot griddle."

Louisiana's mother was a case in point. Zsa-Zsu was twenty-five and working as an exotic dancer in the French Quarter the night Billy flew into New Orleans and tumbled head over heels for her. In the glow of neon lights, they were married. Nine months later and to Billy's delight, Zsa-Zsu presented him with a baby girl. The only thing was, she didn't stick around long enough to even name the child. She was too filled with restless needs that were stifled out there in the middle of the parched Texas landscape. She was drying up. So, with a sizable dissolution check tucked into her garter belt, Zsa-Zsu dashed back to New Orleans and got her old job again.

There had been many other abridged affairs and marriages, but only one other child. Six years before Louisiana was born, Billy had met another young starlet on the rise. That time it was a twenty-two-year-old named Camille, who married him long enough to give him a son and assure for herself a fat divorce settlement that would tide her over the lean years until she took her place among the Hollywood giants. The last anybody heard, Camille was selling real estate in La Jolla.

To compensate for the lack of a mother, their daddy lavished an inordinate amount of attention on his two children. They shared the limelight with him, and through their young years they belonged more to the public than to themselves. Ham and Louisiana shared the uncommon brand of being Billy Boone Bond's children. Despite the years between them, that connection alone had kept them close.

She scanned the ads, then went back and read them all again. That was odd; there had to be one. Ham hadn't missed an issue for the past two years. One hundred and four brief notes to her buried somewhere in the classifieds.

So why was there nothing this time?

Pulling her feet from the desk, she swung the chair around and opened a door on the credenza behind the desk. Inside were several stacks of *Adventures in Warfare*. She pulled out last week's issue. She opened it up and flipped to the classifieds, going straight to the entry she had circled. Ham always had a convoluted way of saying the simplest of things, and he loved codes. But she had to admit this last garbled missive she hadn't been able to figure out. "L.B.: Gunner for hire. Specializes in archeology. The Tiger Den. Go for the truth. Love, H.B." She just didn't get it.

Louisiana stared out the window, wondering. What did it mean? Gunner for hire? Archeology? And what the heck was the Tiger Den? Beyond those questions was why there was no message this week. He had never failed to send one. If he were going on vacation, he would have let her know. What had that boy gotten himself into this time?

Of course, just because he'd been in pickles most of his life didn't necessarily mean he was in one now. Maybe he just forgot to tell her about his vacation. Maybe he wasn't feeling well. Maybe he had grown tired of the correspondence game. Maybe he'd been abducted by pirates! She frowned. Were there pirates in Thailand?

She had always had a bad habit of blowing innocent events all out of proportion. Daddy Bond had teased her that her imagination ran as wild and erratic as a Texas cyclone, tossing up debris everywhere, muddling up the whole darn picture. And here she was, doing it again.

All she needed to do was sit and think about this calmly and logically. This less-than-direct message of Ham's was probably in some way related to his newfound religion. For the past few months, he'd been sending articles to her on Buddhism, and he'd included several of its maxims in his classifieds.

She flipped through several back issues until she found an entry: "This one's it, Louisie. Nirvana, baby." Ham had never been a religious man, and he did not instill much affirmation in Louisiana with that message. She knew he was very much caught up in the Thai culture, but Buddhism? Why, all that self-denial went against everything the Bond name stood for!

Okay, this was ridiculous. If she was worried about him, she should just place a call to his office, inquire as to his health and then everything would be fine. It was really no big deal.

She pressed a button on the phone, reconnecting it, and when she got a tone, dialed direct to Ham's office in Bangkok.

"Bond Publications," the voice on the other end said. The girl spoke English, but the Oriental influence hung like a bamboo parasol over the words.

"Ham Bond, please."

"I sorry. Mr. Bond not here. Who is calling, please."

"This is his sister, Louisiana Bond."

"Oh."

The silence brought a frown to Louisiana's forehead. "Do you know where he is?"

"No. Ah, just a moment, please."

Louisiana could hear a muffled conversation even though the girl had put her hand over the mouthpiece. When she came back on the line, she said, "He not tell us where he is going."

"Did he go on vacation?"

The hesitation lasted too long to be reassuring. "No."

"So you don't know when he will be back?"

In the woman's sigh, Louisiana read a great deal. And this time she did not think her imagination was running wild. "We do not know," the woman said, almost sadly. "He . . . you are really sister?"

"Yes."

"From Texas?"

"Yes. Is something wrong? Has something happened to Ham?"

Her voice lowered, as if she didn't want anyone else in the room to hear. "I do not know. I think—maybe yes."

Louisiana glanced at the magazine on the desk in front of her. "Does the name the Tiger Den mean anything to you?"

There was only a slight pause. "It is bar."

"A bar? A drinking type of bar?"

"Yes. Drinks."

"It's in Bangkok?"

"Yes. On Surawong Road."

A bar. "Would that, by any chance, be a place to find a—a gunner for hire?"

"A gunner. Ah, you mean Gunner? He go there."

"He?"

The woman put her hand over the mouthpiece and mumbled to someone in the room. When she came back, she said, "I go now."

"No, wait," said Louisiana. "You said he. Who is *he?*"

"I say nothing. I go now. Have nice day."

Have nice day. Right. When Louisiana hung up, she was more confused than ever. She reread Ham's message from last week's magazine. *Gunner for hire.* It sounded military, but Ham hadn't been actively involved in soldiering for several years. Injured in a conflict in Afghanistan, he had given up playing war in favor of publishing. Still, there was something warlike about the message. But the girl had said "he." He go there. So it wasn't a gunner. It was a Gunner. And Gunner obviously hung out at a bar called the Tiger Den.

Specializes in archeology. Now that didn't have anything to do with being a soldier. Ham's hobby was archeology. He loved nothing more than to take off on some mysterious dig somewhere. She felt prickles move along her spine. Maybe that was it. He could have been hired to help with a dig. Or did this man, Gunner, specialize in archeology?

And why had he tacked on that *Go for the truth?* What truth? Was Ham telling *her* to go for the truth?

Louisiana leaned forward in the chair and gripped the magazine between her fingers. Her heart was beating fast and she felt a sense of excitement and unrest inch along her veins. This message had meant nothing to her when she'd read it last week. It still didn't make sense, but now she was convinced that Ham had gotten into trouble. Something wasn't right here. She had the notion that her brother was trying to tell her something important, but her brain was just too thick to decipher the code.

Without bothering to save the lease agreement on the computer, she cleared the screen and typed the message he had sent her last week. She then pulled the key words—Gunner, archeology, the Tiger Den, truth—and typed them out. She filled in Ham's possible connection to each word. She tried rearranging them, trying to fit them into some kind of logical order. Finally she sat back in her chair and stared at the computer screen in front of her. She still didn't understand it, but she did know that Ham needed her. Something was going on and she was being called to action.

Pressing the button on her intercom, she spoke to the woman in the adjacent office. ''Mrs. Kruger, I need you to book a flight for me today. Bangkok, Thailand. Yes, I'm going to see Ham. No, of course nothing is wrong. Oh, sure, you'll do fine at the board meeting without me, Mrs. Kruger. You always have. Tell everyone you're me and I can guarantee they'll never know the difference. Most of those old coots haven't opened their eyes in one of those meetings for years. Oh, and make that as early a flight as possible.'' She lifted her finger from the intercom button, signaling an end to the conversation. She looked at the screen once more before clicking off the machine. It was time to pack.

Billy Boone Bond had been a man of action, a man who quickly sized up a situation, then immediately sprang into gear. He had not been one to waver or sit around and chew over a particular quandary. Nor had he ever wasted time looking for alternate plans in case plan A failed. If he had a problem, he took care of it. And he fully expected to succeed first time around.

Despite her occasional self-doubts, Louisiana Bond was very much Billy Boone Bond's daughter.

A savage place! as holy and enchanted
As e'er beneath a waning moon
was haunted
By woman wailing for her demon lover!

Chapter Two

Pedestrians sloshed ankle-deep in mud across Surawong Road. Trousers were rolled, skirts were raised,
shoes were held in hand. Small children rode high in
their parents' arms, oblivious to the fact that Bangkok was sinking in its own mud, and that if nothing
were done about it, this city of bright silk and golden
palaces and floating markets would very soon be invaded and washed over by the Gulf of Thailand.

The evening sky above the city was gray and heavy,
promising more of the same weather. It was Septem-
ber, the monsoon season. The spinning wheels from
cars and motorcycles and three-wheeled *samlors*
sprayed water over the sidewalks and into the open
doorways of small shops. Everyone made the best of
a situation that was unchangeable.

With her khaki slacks rolled to the knees and her
safari boots and socks clutched in her arms, Louisiana Bond pushed open the door to the Tiger Den and
stepped inside, prepared for anything. Well, almost
anything. A half-naked woman mixing margaritas was
one thing she had failed to anticipate.

She also had not expected to be the only other woman in the place. But Louisiana was used to that. She had grown up in a man's world, circling the globe with Billy on his frequent business trips and adventurous jaunts. She had been included in his all-male parleys and amusements, while the other wives and daughters had been left at home or at least in the company of one another. She had even been to quite a few rough bars in her time, for Billy Boone had preferred grit and substance to glitter and pomp. But she had to admit that this joint, being the kind of place that sticks to the bottom of your shoes, was one that even Daddy Bond might have tagged a hellhole.

She smiled cheerfully at the stone-chiseled faces of the men who had turned on their bar stools to stare at her, but she wisely refrained from a saucy, "Hi, y'all." She wondered which one of these men, if any, would be able to shed some light on Ham's mysterious message and disappearance.

"Okie from Muskogee" played from the jukebox, and the smell of sweat and booze in the place was thick enough to cut with a knife. The woman behind the counter discreetly pulled her dress back up over her torso and poured the margaritas into tall glasses, then plunked them down on the counter. No one picked them up. They were all looking at the woman in the doorway. Louisiana wished now that she had bought one of those camouflage outfits from Neiman's commando collection. She would have fit right in with this ragtag bunch of misfits.

Louisiana, old girl, she told herself. *You have never been anywhere that you didn't fit right in. You have always belonged. But I've got an inkling that maybe— just maybe—you don't belong in this place.* Still, she knew what Billy Boone would have done in this situation. He would have marched right up to the bar, eased his big Texas frame down onto a bar stool and ordered himself a shot of Yukon Jack.

Louisiana marched over to the counter, set on doing the same thing. Except that there were no vacant bar stools. So she just stood there with boots in hand and smiled patiently until one of the men, whose face was as corrugated as a farmer's bean field, was shamed into giving up his place.

A younger man behind the bar held a polishing rag only inches above the counter, all duty suspended while he processed the woman sitting before him. In fact, it seemed to her as if the whole place were suspended in timeless stop-action play. Only Merle Haggard's twangy tune played on.

She took the quiet moment to accustom herself to the place. All around the bar were hundreds of pictures of a man, younger in some photos and older in others, posing with a colorful array of characters. There was a stairway leading to the second floor. All the tables and booths were jammed at this hour of evening. The margarita hostess had gone back to her patrons at the far end of the bar. By the time Louisiana finished looking the place over, most of the men had returned to the business of drinking, but a few were still gawking at her.

"I'm looking for someone who might go by the name of Gunner. Do you know anyone like that?"

The male bartender said nothing. He was back to wiping up the bar. But the guy on her left leaned close and said, "Ah, honey, now what you want to go and look up somebody like that for? I'm the only one you're gonna need." His neck was as thick as his head and he wore a T-shirt that read Mercenaries—They Just Go to Hell to Regroup.

Louisiana smiled blandly and turned back to the bartender.

But a guy on her right then leaned her way, speaking around her to the one in the T-shirt. "I think we oughta buy this little gal a drink, don't you?" He stuck his face up close to hers and said, "What'll you have, darlin'—glass of white wine?"

She studied the offensive curiosity on her right, taking note of the tattoos that covered every square inch of his arms, the lizard-design T-shirt on his hard frame, the stubbly beard on his chin and the capped tooth that gleamed brightly when he grinned at her. She turned back to the bartender. "You have any Yukon Jack?"

He stopped moving the rag. "I hear you right?"

"Canadian," she said. "High proof. You have any?"

"We've got everything here a drinkin' man needs."

"Good," she said. "I'll have a double shot. In a clean glass, if you don't mind."

She glanced pointedly at the beers the two men beside her were drinking, then smiled to herself when they practically fell over the bar in a rush to order double shots of whiskey for themselves.

The bartender reached for a glass on the counter, flicked it sideways to get rid of the cigarette butt that sat in the bottom of it, then dipped it into a sink of brown water. He reached under the counter for the bottle, poured in two fingers and set it on the counter in front of her. "That clean enough for you?"

Louisiana kept the surge of nausea at bay and gritted her teeth. "Perfect." She watched him fill glasses for her two friends at the bar, then she picked up hers, raised it in a silent toast to them and knocked it down in one swallow.

On her left, GI Joe was gawking at her as if he'd never seen a woman before in his life. The truth of the matter was, he had just never seen a woman who looked like Louisiana Bond down a shot of Yukon Jack without falling over in a dead faint.

"Nice shirt," she said to him, then to the bartender, "Sugar, you want to pour me another one, please?"

The bartender chuckled and reached for the bottle. "You bet. What's the matter with you guys? Can't keep up with a girl?"

They both downed their drinks in quick gulps and set them back on the counter for a refill.

"As I was saying," Louisiana began when she once again had a full glass. "I'm looking for someone named Gunner. You guys know anyone by that name?"

They watched her polish off her second glass, then they did the same. "What's it to you?" Tattoos asked.

She held the glass out to the bartender. "It's personal."

They held their glasses out also, but she could tell that GI Joe was having trouble staying on the bar stool as he slurred, "He owe ya money or somethin'?"

"No."

"Well, we don't know him."

She drank down the third shot and caught the quick exchange of glances that passed between the two men and the bartender. "Really," she said.

The bartender shrugged. "Tell you what, honey. You leave me your name and address and if—well, if anybody by that name should happen to drop in, I'll tell him you're looking for him.''

She reached into her purse for a pen, grabbed a paper napkin from the counter and wrote her name and the name of the hotel where she was staying. She handed the napkin to the bartender. He perused it with a frown.

"Louisiana Bond," she said, in case he couldn't read. In a place like this, one could never tell. "I'm at the Oriental."

"Bond," he mused. "I know a guy named Bond."

"I have a brother named Ham Bond. I think he comes here every so often. You know him?"

"Ham!" the bartender said. "He's your brother!"

"Yes." She glanced sideways in time to watch Tattoos ooze from the stool and land belly-up on the floor of the bar.

On her left, GI Joe was staring at her dully, his glass held in his hand but tipped sideways at a sixty-five-degree angle so that the whiskey ran out and formed a pool on the counter. "Ham Bond's sister?" he barely managed. "Holy sh—" He dropped his head to the bar and passed out cold.

"Hey, Duck," the bartender yelled toward the back. "Get out here. I've got somebody I want you to meet."

After a moment, a man—the same man who graced the hundreds of photos on the wall—strode out from a back room. He stopped for a second and stared at the woman sitting at his bar. Then he pushed back his panama hat, adjusted his bolo tie and clomped in his boots over to a spot directly in front of her. He peered at her with a narrowed, thoughtful gaze, looked down once at the drop of whiskey left in her glass, then slapped his hand down on the bar and said, "Yukon Jack, huh?"

She lifted the glass and drank it down, smiling as she set the empty glass back on the counter. He squinted his eyes, watching for a reaction. When she didn't show the one he expected, he straightened up and bellowed loudly, "Hey, everybody, we've got us a new hobo!"

"Ham's sister," said the bartender.

The man in the panama hat slapped her on the back, nearly knocking her off the stool, and said, "Ham Bond's sister. How long you been in town, little lady?" He handed her glass over to the bartender for another shot.

Louisiana didn't want another round of whiskey, but she knew at this point she couldn't call it quits. If she did, she'd never get the information she had come for. Daddy Bond had taught her a long time ago that if you want something from people, you've got to get down on their level. Glancing at the two drunks who were passed out beside her, she wasn't really all that sure she wanted to go that far, but if it was the only way to find the man she was looking for . . .

"Got in today, sugar," she said.

"This one's on me, honey," said the man in the panama hat, handing the glass back to her. "I'm just tickled pink to see you. I love meeting new crossroaders. Been meeting new ones and drinking with the old ones now for—well, hell, since the end of '71. That was when I got run out of East Pakistan, ya know. Yep, went on a fifty-four-day drunk, and when I sobered up I found myself in Bangkok."

"So what did you do then?"

He grinned and said, "I opened this bar. Seemed the thing to do." He pushed his hat back even farther and stuck out his hand. "Duck Tyger at your service."

Her hand met his. "Louisiana Bond."

"You in all the way from Texas?"

"You bet," she said a bit breathlessly as he crunched her knuckles. She was accustomed to Texans' boisterous enthusiasm, but this man outdid them all. And now everyone in the bar seemed to join the fray. Big burly guys in olive-drab T-shirts were coming over to slap her on the back and pump her hand as if she were just one of the boys. It was obvious that Ham had made a few friends in this place.

The bartender set the full glass in front of her. "She said she thinks Ham comes here every so often."

Duck laughed heartily. "Ham doesn't come here every so often, honey. Ham damn near lives here."

As close as she and her brother were, there was quite a bit, she gathered, that she didn't know about him.

"Yeah," said Duck, "he started out back in the seventies, coming here for hobo night whenever he was in town. That was when I used to have hobo night, ya know. Not anymore, though."

"Hobo night?"

"Friday night. That was the night I used to give away food. A lot of ex-Nam guys were always hanging around, out of work." He jabbed Tattoos with the toe of his boot, but the guy didn't budge. "Not like these fellas now. They got more work out there'n they know what to do with. Everybody hates everybody nowadays. Wars here, feuds there. World's a dang mess, if you ask me."

"Drop-kick Me, Jesus, Through the Goalpost of Life" was now playing on the jukebox and Duck looked as if he had plenty more to tell her.

"Anyways," he was saying, "I used to put up a spread, nothin' fancy, ya know, but there was all the spaghetti and salad you could eat. Or sometimes bacon and beans. Ham used to come around between jobs and fill up his gut. 'Course, I don't do that anymore. The damn hippies started coming in and eating me out of house and home. Didn't mind feeding 'em too much. But when they started takin' up space in my bar—takin' up space where good drinkers ought to be sittin'—that's when I had to say *whoa* to hobo night."

"When was the last time you saw Ham?"

Duck looked puzzled. "I told you, he's in here all the time. Still comes in for hobo beans, French bread and bacon. I serve that upstairs. Drink up, girl. You're lookin' parched." He rubbed his chin. "'Course, now that I think about it, I haven't seen him for a week or so. Nope, sure haven't. Now I wonder where he snuck off to."

"That, sugar, is what I'd like to know," she said.

He grinned. "Well, when you find that rascal, you tell him to get in here and see old Duck. I'm pretty sure he owes me money."

It was obvious to Louisiana that Ham's friends didn't know much about his background or his financial situation. "Pretty sure?" She laughed.

"Honey, everybody who spends any time here does."

He started to move on down the bar to talk to his other customers, but she stopped him. "I'm also looking for another man, Duck. One who goes by the name of Gunner. Ham told me to look him up if I was ever in town.''

There was a quick flicker of surprise in Duck's eyes. He glanced at a man seated two stools down from Louisiana, then laughed again. He slapped the man on the back and said, ''Looks like you've got yourself a visitor.''

The man didn't look up. He kept his eyes directed toward the wall behind the bar and slowly sipped a beer. His hair was a medium shade of brown and neatly styled, unlike that of her two has-been drinking buddies. Since he hadn't yet bothered to look in her direction, she had to admire the clean straight lines of his profile. He didn't have the battered, slightly bloated look of the two men who had been sitting beside her. And, unlike them, he was wearing brown cotton slacks and an expensive sport coat over an oxford shirt. On his feet he wore loafers with no socks.

Louisiana couldn't help but stare at him. He was totally incongruous with the surroundings. He looked nothing like the other men in the bar. He had a relaxed elegance about him, while the rest of the patrons looked as if they'd just crawled out of some mosquito-infested swamp.

He quietly finished his beer, and when it was empty he swung his stool slowly so that he was facing her. With an impassive kind of expression, he said, ''You lookin' for me?''

His voice was low and well modulated without a trace of an accent that she could determine. ''You're Gunner?''

He nodded.

''And you've been sitting there the whole time?''

''For a while.''

Upper midwest, she thought. *Iowa or Michigan, maybe.* "Since before I came in?"

"Yes."

"Didn't you hear me asking about you?"

"I heard."

Her mouth tightened. "I see."

His gaze swept over her in quick assessment. "You really Ham's sister?"

He was even more handsome than his profile had suggested, with brown eyes and enough character lines to place him somewhere in the range of late thirties or early forties. But despite his good looks, she was perturbed by the suspicious tone. "Why would I lie about something like that, Mr. Gunner?"

"The name's Gunner. Not Mister. Just Gunner. And I don't know why you would lie. You tell me."

She didn't bother to answer that. "Do you know my brother? Ham?"

"I know him."

She glanced around the noisy bar. Duck was proudly showing a group of guys the scars on his chest where he'd had a run-in with an angry Bengal.

One Rambo clone stopped and asked the bartender if they were showing the Vietnam movies upstairs. The bartender said they were and the guy shoved his way through the crowd and up the stairs.

On the jukebox, cowboy twang had given way to an Al Jolson song.

Louisiana looked back at the handsome man who was still sitting two bar stools away and said, "He told me to look you up."

"What for?"

She glanced around once again, this time to see if anyone was listening in on their conversation. No one was. The bartender was busy at the other end of the long bar and her two drinking partners appeared to be out for the count. "Well, now, sugar," she said to Gunner, "I'm not sure."

He studied her for a long moment and his eyes seemed to miss nothing. He finally said, "That was quite a show you put on with the whiskey."

She left the latest full glass untouched on the counter. "Not quite as entertaining as the show I saw when I first came in."

Gunner glanced at the hostess who had performed the topless margarita ceremony. He looked back at Louisiana. "You do that sort of thing, too?"

She shrugged. "Well, now, darlin', there's always a first time for everything, isn't there?"

They sat quietly appraising each other, intrigued but cautious.

"Where did you learn to drink like that?" he asked.

"From my daddy."

"Billy Boone Bond."

"That's right. Ham must have told you about him."

"I do read, Miss Bond. But you're right. Ham filled in where the press left off." His eyes made another quick pass over her. "So Billy Boone taught you how to drink."

"Yep."

"Among other things, he must have been a good teacher."

"He was."

Gunner twirled the empty bottle of Singha between his hands. "What else did he teach you?"

"To like everybody and to trust nobody."

"Sounds like good advice."

"It's served me well." Louisiana watched him twirl the empty bottle. It gave the impression of a man who was somewhat impatient, perhaps a man in a hurry, and yet he didn't seem primed to rush off anywhere. "Listen, uh, Gunner. Could we go somewhere— someplace where we can talk in private?"

"About what?"

"About Ham."

His eyes drifted over her lazily. She had the feeling that he was peeling away the layers of her clothes to see what lay beneath. "What's there to talk about?"

He was a cool one, he was, inscrutability behind an iron mask. But she sensed something alive beneath it, something physical and perhaps dangerous. Heat struck like a match tip against her nerve endings. "I think he's in trouble."

Gunner's fingers tightened almost imperceptibly around the empty bottle. "Well, it's that kind of town."

"I think he may be in danger."

He let go of the bottle and his hand flattened against the top of the bar. "Look, Miss Bond. I said I know the guy, that's all. I mean, I don't keep track of—"

"He said you specialized in archeology."

His eyes lingered on her, missing nothing. After a moment, they narrowed and the lines of his forehead drew together in a frown. He glanced around, his eyes quick and calculating. When he looked back at her, she felt a kind of warning implicit in his gaze and his words. "There aren't too many private spots in Bangkok. Not with five million people swarming the place."

"We could go to my hotel," she suggested.

"To your room?"

She straightened on the stool. "I wasn't implying—"

His eyes centered on her mouth for only the briefest second. "Neither was I. I'm talking about privacy. Your room's no good."

"You mean...?" She hadn't thought about the possibility that her suite would not be private. Was he hinting that it might be bugged? No one knew she was here. And even if they did, why would anyone bother to listen in on *her* conversations? She didn't have that kind of celebrity. The man was obviously suffering from a bad case of tabloid paranoia. "There's a lobby in the Oriental Hotel."

"The Author's Lounge?"

"Yes," she said. "Will that do?"

"That'll be fine."

She let go of the breath she had been holding, suspecting that the man had as much to do with her tension as her brother's disappearance did. She had been charmed up and down every continent in her thirty-four years and was immune to most male ploys. This man either had no new tricks to play or he was using ones she had never seen before. Whichever it was, she felt as if she had just been raked over live coals.

The bartender walked by and she asked him how much she owed. When she had settled her tab and Gunner had paid for his beer, she picked up her boots and socks from the floor and they left the bar together. Behind her, she could hear Duck Tyger regaling the remaining "hobos" with stories of his days back in the forties when he was working the Alcan in Prince Rupert.

Gunner steered her out into the wet Bangkok evening, and when the door closed behind her on the Tiger Den she said, "Goodness, why was everyone so protective of you in there? You hiding out from somebody?"

He shrugged. "Just habit. Most of those guys don't want to be found."

"What about you?"

"You found me, didn't you?"

While he hailed a taxi, Louisiana studied him closely. "Tell me something," she said. "If Duck hadn't let me know who you were, would you have said anything?"

"Probably not."

A taxi eased into the curb. "You wouldn't have been the least bit aroused by curiosity?" she asked.

He opened the back door and his eyes slid down her in one long, slow sweep. When his gaze locked with hers, he murmured in a low voice, "Yeah, I would have been aroused."

His eyes, like the night, were dark and hot and steamy, and she absorbed the intensity from them as if her body and mind were a yielding sponge. But she knew she had to resist this feeling. She had to force herself to remember why it was that she was here in Thailand. Ham was in some kind of trouble. After her visit to his office this afternoon, she was more certain than ever that something had happened to him. He needed her and he had sent her to find this man. And until she knew why, she had to keep a safe distance.

No matter how handsome he was or how tempting his voice and eyes were, she knew virtually nothing about him. Because of where she had found him, he was probably a soldier of fortune. By whatever means it had taken, he had survived. So despite Ham's message and her desire to make sure that he was safe, Louisiana sensed, intuitively, that this man called Gunner was not a man to be trusted.

It was a miracle of rare device,
A sunny pleasure dome with caves of ice!

Chapter Three

The Author's Lounge was deserted and quiet at this time of night. A vestige of the old original hotel, its ambience of white wicker beneath potted bamboo and palm, along with its exotic blend of teas, was steeped in memories of years gone by.

Gunner held a glass of Scotch between both hands and studied the woman who was sitting in the wicker chair across from him. She was drinking Ceylon tea to counteract the effects of all that Yukon Jack. "So why me?" he asked.

"I don't know," she said. "I thought you could tell me."

She was the type of woman you would never get tired of looking at; he had to give her that. She had long strawberry blond hair, and her skin was as ripe and smooth as a Texas peach. But her eyes, the color of Burmese jade, radiated an intelligence and a sense of determination that made him wary. "No."

"Ham wanted me to see you. He wanted me to ask for your help. I mean, it's all right here."

He looked down at the copies of *Adventures in Warfare* that were on the table between them. She had shown him several weeks' worth of classified notes, including the last one that mentioned his name. *It was*

all right there, she said. No way. In his line of work,
no one ever laid it *all* out on the table. One or two
cards were always kept in hand. But what about
Louisiana Bond? What was she holding back? And
what and how much had Ham told her that she wasn't
telling him?

He waved his hand over the clippings. "I don't
know what any of this means. You say there's a message in there. Well, what is it?"

"I'm not sure, but I know he's trying to tell me
something."

"Like what?"

He watched her set down her cup of tea and reach
for one of the magazines. She had an economy of
movements, as if there was not a moment in life to
fritter away, and yet each motion was wrapped in flu-
idity and grace. The magazine lay open in her lap.
"Gunner for hire. That's you, hon."

He shrugged.

"The Tiger Den. That's where I found you." She
smiled imperiously. "I assume you're the only man
named Gunner who hangs out at the Tiger Den."

Gunner took a long drink of Scotch and then fixed
her with a steady gaze. "Could be dozens of us."

"Do you have another name?"

"No."

"I see. What you're saying, then, is that you don't
have one that you're going to share with me."

"Something like that."

She looked back at the magazine. "Do you specialize in archeology?"

"No."

She frowned. "Ham is sort of an archeology buff.
But you already know that, don't you?"

He shrugged. "So I've heard."

Frustrated by his total unwillingness to cooperate with her, she pursed her lips. "Then why, darlin', do you think he would have mentioned it to me?"

His gaze left her eyes and settled on her mouth. She was wearing red lipstick that matched perfectly the color of her fingernails. He wished he would stop noticing these little details about her. He also wished that she would stop asking so many questions. "Hell if I know...darlin'."

She sat back, drained from the mental gymnastics. The tea tasted smooth and warm, and night sounds drifted in from the open doorway, a gentle contrast to their conversation. "How do you and Ham know each other?"

He looked down into his Scotch. "We've done some jobs together."

"Jobs."

"Yes."

"Where?"

He shrugged. "Around. Laos, Rhodesia, Afghanistan."

He could tell she was just itching to ask him more about that, but something made her drop it for the moment. Of course, he figured any woman who flew across the world after one cryptic message wasn't the type to let it drop for long.

"When did you see him last?"

He hesitated, wondering how much she already knew and how much more he should tell her. He had to tell her enough to satisfy her curiosity, but not enough to make her want to stick around and dig for more. "A little over two weeks ago."

"Where?"

"At the Tiger Den."

She continued to watch him and he knew he was being analyzed. She was trying to put it all into some kind of logical order. He could have told her that logic had very little to do with it, but she probably wouldn't have listened. "And you two were just having a boys' night out on the town?"

"Something like that."

She had picked up her cup of tea and, as she held it to her lips, she was watching him over the rim. He wished he knew what to make of her. With all those "sugars" and "darlin's" dropping from her pretty mouth, she brought to mind warm summer afternoons on a porch swing. She was soft and sexy, and the engine that lay deep in his body was starting to rumble. On the other hand, she was butting in where she had no business. She interrogated him as if he were some kind of war criminal. She drank whiskey like a sailor. She wore safari boots. For the life of him he could not get a bead on her.

"What kind of work do you do?" she asked when he didn't offer anything more.

"Oh, this and that."

"This and that," she repeated with a slight smile.

"Yes. I travel around a bit."

"Like Ham?"

"I suppose."

"That's interesting." She took a sip of tea and then cocked her head, never taking her eyes off of him. "Until a few years ago, Ham was a soldier of fortune. Is that what you are?"

He finished his drink and set it on the table. He tried to convince himself that he was not enjoying this conversation with her, but the revving motor within told him otherwise. In another place and another time, he might have followed his body's inclination to play the parlor game with her. If she were not Ham Bond's sister, and if she were not here on this particular mission . . . if he had simply met her at a party, he would probably have asked her to come out and play. But it was not to be. Not with this one. The stakes were too high.

"I don't much like fighting. You can get hurt doing that sort of thing."

She looked less than convinced and added, "My brother's in publishing. Are you some sort of reporter?"

"I'm a deal maker, Miss Bond."

She cocked her head and studied him. "What kind of deal maker?"

"All aboveboard, I assure you. My days of sneaking around jungles at night are over. Look." He sighed. "Here's what I do. If someone wants to expand his business into Thailand, I can help. I find banks, lawyers, employees, office buildings, help with the governmental red tape. Or if some friendly government contractor wants five hundred ditchdiggers taken from Timbuktu to Kalamazoo and they have to pass through Thailand, I make it easy for them." He shrugged. "That's what I do."

Her gaze narrowed on him, still unconvinced. He hadn't fooled her for a minute.

"You know," she said slowly. "From the time I was little bitty, my daddy would take me out into the oil patch with him. There were cattle roaming everywhere and little iron pumps going up and down. And you know something, sugar? I learned real early on how to spot all those bull patties lying out there in the pastures. Why, I could sprint two hundred yards and miss every one of them.''

His gaze swept over her lithe, pampered body, then landed squarely on those shrewd green eyes. He realized, suddenly, how very different she was from most women he knew. ''Nice story. You tell that one at the afternoon bridge parties?''

He watched the transformation of her face. Her chin shot forward, her head tilted at an arrogant angle, her arms crossed in front of her. Here was a woman who, because of her money, probably didn't have to take a lot of guff from people. Deference, he felt sure, surrounded her.

''Darlin','' she said in a voice too soft to match the cool expression. ''My daddy taught me how to survive in a man's world. He neglected the more feminine things, like afternoon bridge parties. Now…'' She sighed. ''Do you suppose that you and I could get past this adversarial relationship?''

''You can go back to Texas and we can send each other greeting cards.''

''I can't do that, Gunner.'' Her eyes locked with his. ''Something is very wrong here. Ham is in trouble. And I don't think you would have agreed to talk to me tonight if you didn't know something about this.''

''Ham's been in trouble before.''

''I'm sure he has. But this time he obviously needs help or he never would have written this message. No one has seen him or heard from him in almost a week.''

''How do you know that?''

''I went to his office today. His staff was worried. Oh, they tried to be nonchalant about it all. Said he was probably lying on a beach somewhere up in Pattaya. But I'm a very good judge of that sort of thing, and they were definitely worried. And two days ago when I called, the girl who answered his office phone told me she thought he was in trouble."

She was right, thought Gunner. *Ham is in trouble.* But there was certainly nothing new about that. "I wouldn't know where to begin."

She pursed her lips. "A deal maker like you? With your contacts?"

"What's in it for me?"

Her mouth tightened. "I was wondering when we were going to get down to brass tacks. At least you're not going to feign disinterest in my money."

Something began to growl inside of him, but he wasn't sure if it was anger or lust. "Well, that's us mercenaries for you. We don't know how to feign. We've got the social graces of fry cooks."

Her gaze drifted over the expensive jacket and slacks, the neatly trimmed hair, the straight white teeth. "What's your going rate?"

"For finding missing brothers? Well, I'll have to get back to you on that. Tell you what, I'll work you up an estimate."

"You do that." A ruthless glint flickered for a split second in her eyes, just long enough to tell him that this woman was used to playing hardball. But the fight left her face and weariness replaced it. Her eyes closed briefly and he felt an unfamiliar stab of something akin to sympathy.

"It's been a long day," she finally said, opening her eyes. "A long flight."

He took the hint and stood, but before taking his leave, he needed to reestablish the pecking order and issue a fair warning of his own. He leaned down and rested his hand on the back of her chair. His face was close enough that he caught the scent of the soap she had used. Her green eyes, awash with fatigue and a hint of moisture, unconsciously beckoned him. "I'm sure your daddy taught you a great deal, Miss Bond. But I just want to make it clear that here, in this man's world, we play for keeps." He pushed off from the chair and said, "Now you sleep well, Louisiana Bond."

She stared up at him. "I always do."

Without another word, Gunner walked out the back door, through the hotel gardens and on toward the river. He followed the path down to the banks, where he stopped and stared moodily over the muddy *klong,* known as Chao Phya—the River of Kings. The moon slid from behind its cloud cover and cast a pale reflection over the water. It was a warm night, vaporous and veiled, the kind he liked best. The rain had let up, but he knew the monsoon was not yet over. He had lived here for so long he could feel the rhythm of the seasons within him, a cadence that rose and fell with every breath he took.

There had been a time when he had thought about going back to the States to live, but no longer. He was content here. He had found his own rhythm. And while there were times when he thought about and even longed for the American way of life—sometimes including in that vision the feel of an American woman—he knew he would not leave. This was home now.

"You scare her off?"

Gunner turned toward the sound. A man wearing a red bandanna stood beside him. "I'm not sure, but, dammit, Bruno, do you feel it necessary to creep through the bushes all the time?"

"Must get rid of her" came the rough reply.

"We will." Gunner looked back over the Chao Phya, then heard the click of a new magazine shoved into the chamber of a gun. Gunner turned toward the man holding a loaded handgun. "You're too impatient, Bruno."

"She is beautiful woman," said Bruno in his gruff, heavily accented voice. "She make you weak."

Gunner glanced sharply at Bruno, then smiled and shrugged it off. "Maybe." He reached over and grasped the hand that was holding the pistol, guiding it back into the holster inside the man's jacket. "You could use a little of that weakness yourself. Now that's Ham Bond's sister in there. Just keep an eye on her, okay?"

"You still want to follow through with the plan?" asked Bruno.

"Yes, we keep to the schedule. Inform the others, will you?"

Bruno nodded, but added, "I don't like this business with Ham Bond. And the sister...she could cause trouble."

From the reaction in his body just at the thought of Louisiana Bond, Gunner felt trouble coming his way. In spades. He didn't want to mention that to Bruno. He let his gaze swim back over the river. A lonely sampan floated downstream in the dark, moving with the flow of sludge. "We'll just have to make sure she doesn't."

*And from this chasm, with ceaseless
turmoil seething,
As if this earth in fast thick pants
were breathing*

Chapter Four

The hot sticky night closed around them. The smell of
the dense teak forest was wet and thick in their noses.
A cloud of steam rose from the spongy jungle floor.
Ham took the old abbot's arm and urged him forward. "Po, please, you've got to hurry."

"I try. But—my leg."

"I know." Ham found a leafy spot. "Here, we'll
rest a minute." He helped the old man to sit down. As
soon as he was comfortable and the statue he had been
carrying was laid in the grass at his side, Po pressed the
palms of his hands and fingers together and closed his
eyes. A single tone, low and rich, came from the man's
throat.

Ham tried to conjure up a state of blissful repose,
but he was finding it difficult. He was able to do it in
the temple with Po. But out here in the jungle, the
soldier in him was too strong. To kill, even in self-
defense, was wrong, taught Po. Man must transcend
the need to win. But how could Ham not protect himself? How could he not save his friend? The mist
within his own mind held him captive. He looked to
the abbot and wished to find the peace that the older

man had found. But a good soldier always knew his own limitations.

When the abbot once again opened his eyes, Ham said, "Are you ready? Can you go on now?"

"Yes, a bit, I think."

Ham reached around Po's back and grasped him under the arm, lifting the weight off his hurt leg. "We'll try to find a safer place to stop soon."

They snaked their way up the thick, forested slope, Ham half carrying the abbot, while the older man clutched the statue of the Enlightened One, the Buddha, to his chest. Plain by comparison with most of Thailand's religious symbols, this one was made solely of jade. It weighed heavily in the old man's arms, but he would not part with it. It was not only ancient, its value was beyond measure.

And it was the reason they were both running for their lives in the depths of this steamy jungle. Ham had discovered the statue a few weeks ago. And through Po he had learned just how valuable it really was. But others wanted it, too. And last week they had stolen the statue and kidnapped Po to have it and the store of its vast secrets. Ham had been looking for the old man for days. He had rescued Po yesterday from the kidnappers. But Ham, always a realist, knew that they still had many rivers to cross.

The two men moved on like spirits through the night. A thin rivulet cut through the trail and soon they stepped into a mist-filled clearing. Nestled in the haze was a bamboo shelter perched high on poles to protect it against the monsoons. They made their way into the clearing, and Ham silently sighed with relief. Po couldn't go much farther and neither could he. They were both very tired. They needed rest. Tomorrow they could follow the river down from the mountains. Maybe in a couple of days they would reach Bangkok and this nightmare would come to an end.

"Over there," he said to Po. "It looks deserted. We can sleep there for the night."

The abbot's weight sagged in relief against him.

They stepped forward, then stopped when the unmistakable clicking sound of rifle bolts echoed in the humid wall of heat around them. From the trees to the side of them stepped four men, three Americans dressed in camouflage and combat boots, and their Thai leader dressed in a silk shirt and expensive trousers.

"You going somewhere, Captain Bond?" one of the Americans asked with an ugly sneer.

Defeat washed through Ham's body, weighting him down. He had failed. He had thought he could save Po and rescue the statue. He had thought he could keep the secret from falling into the thieves' hands. He had wanted nothing more than to transport the jade Buddha back to the temple with Po, where they would both remain safe and contained. But he had failed. Miserably. He glanced at the leader of the men. "Doesn't look like it, Tak," he said wearily.

Two of the Americans laughed and reached for the abbot, yanking the statue from his hands. Tak grasped the collar of Po's robe. "We're not through with you yet, old man. I believe you still have something to show us."

One of the soldiers prodded Ham with his rifle. "What about him? What do you want us to do with him?"

Tak's mouth stretched into a lopsided grin. "I know just the thing," he said slowly. "A fitting end for

Captain Bond." The smile widened. "He can go the way of the ancient martyrs."

Ham had lived by the sword for many years and now, he supposed, it was only fitting that he die by the sword. He had fought alongside three of these men many years before. But they had allowed themselves to be corrupted by the man in the silk shirt—Tak, minister of public works, a man whose political and cultural obligations had been twisted to satisfy his own lustful greed. He would aid in the destruction of his own country if it would enhance his personal wealth. And these three men with him had been sucked in by his hollow promises of wealth and power.

So Ham knew their threats were not bluffs. They were deadly serious.

Last week he had sent a classified message to his sister. It had been done only as a last resort, a signal from a panicked brain, a kind of insurance policy just in case something happened to him. He could trust her with the Buddha's secret. Now he wished he hadn't sent it. After all, he should be able to handle this. And, of course, he hadn't even hinted to her the other operation involving Tak. No one, not even family members, was to know the truth about that part of his job. It was the code he lived by. The code demanded of him.

Maybe he had known somehow that this would not go the way he wanted. Maybe that was why he had sent Louisiana the message. Somehow he had glimpsed a slice of his future and had seen that he would fail. In his panic, his sister had seemed his only hope. Now he knew he had made a terrible mistake. As gutsy and clever as she was, this was no place for

someone like her. One martyr in a family was more
than enough.

"I am sorry, Po," he said to the sad little abbot. *I'm
sorry, Louisie,* he said to himself, then he took a deep
breath of the hot, wet night, realizing that it could very
well be his last.

IT WAS MORNING. Bangkok. Tak studied the stylized
dance of magic between two men inside the boxing
ring. With grace and style, Tak's man leapt, swinging
his foot in a high, smooth arc until it met with a crack
against his opponent's ribs. The struck boxer winced,
but his arm shot out with a returning blow to the current champion's face.

When the practice match was over, the two boxers
turned to Tak and, with gloves pressed together at chin
height, honored him with a bow.

"Lim is good," said Tak to one of the three Thai
men seated beside him. "See that he is well paid."

"And if he loses the fight?"

Tak slowly turned his head, his eyes fixed implaca-
bly on the apprehensive man beside him. He said
nothing, but the young man felt his bones shrink beneath his skin and, with a subservient bow, palms together, quietly slinked away.

"And now," said Tak to the man on his right, "tell
me about the girl."

"It is the sister of Mr. Bond."

Tak was quiet for a moment, looking down at the
floor with his palms pressed together and resting
against pursed lips. "And she is here to see her
brother?"

"She went to his office. We were told that she was asking questions about where he was, when he was last heard from, questions she should not be asking."

"About the Buddha or about the...other matter?" Unfortunately, thought Tak, those meddlesome Americans had found out about the other matter. All of it. The slaves and the rubies. How they had found out, he didn't know. But they had somehow learned of his operation and were on his trail. He was going to have to get the rubies out of the country before they got their hands on them. As for the slaves, maybe he would have to kill them. He didn't want a trail for the Americans to follow. He had been using the Cambodians as slaves on his farm for many years now. It had been so easy to obtain them and force them to cultivate his rice fields. Easy, that is, until the Americans butted in. And now they even wanted to move in on his rubies. His rubies, dammit!

"She mentioned nothing about the rubies or about the slaves," the man said, then shifted uneasily. "But—I, uh..."

"Something you want to say?"

"It is about the Buddha."

Tak studied the young man with amusement. "You seem to have some worries."

The man squirmed under Tak's amused stare. "Yes."

"And what are these worries?"

"It—it is the secrets of the jade Buddha that worry me."

Tak smiled. "Ah. And why is that?"

"You know the legends. You—you know what happens to men who tamper with the treasures of the gods. They say it will bring much unhappiness upon one's house."

Tak laughed, but the young man sensed no mirth in the sound. He stared in fear at his boss.

"There is no place," said Tak slowly, "for a man of foolish superstitions and fear in my operation. Do you understand this?"

"Yes, Tak. I—I am sorry."

"Good. Go now and bring me some tea."

"Yes, Tak."

When he was gone, Tak turned his cold eyes on the last man. "I want no fools in my operation. You must kill him."

"Yes, Tak, I will do that."

"And as for Miss Bond—"

Sweat had formed upon the man's brow. "Yes?"

Tak's eyes narrowed in cold calculation, and then he smiled. "Bring an end to her questions."

THE PRESS OF A SMALL button beside Louisiana's bed brought coffee, croissants and cheese. A bouquet of fresh-cut flowers graced the table on the terrace, where she had decided to eat her breakfast.

An uncertain sun kissed the surface of the Chao Phya River below her. According to the brochure that lay on the credenza inside the room, the towering bee-hive structure, silhouetted against the mist-shrouded sky on the opposite bank, was Wat Arun, the Temple of Dawn.

Sipping her hot coffee, Louisiana thought about how little she knew of this country and its people. They were a blend of Thai, Burmese, Chinese, Indian and Malaysian. She knew that its religions were equally diverse. There were Buddhists, Moslems and

Sikhs. Beyond that, she knew very little. Ham had written small blurbs about the country, and his magazine had featured various articles about the land and its inhabitants, but, in truth, she had paid little attention. Was it that she had been too busy to care? Or was it that she knew Ham so well? He was always flying off on tangents—new wars, new causes, new life-styles. She hadn't paid attention to this one because she hadn't expected it to last.

In a way, she envied him. She always had. He had never felt it necessary to please anyone but himself. He had never felt the burdensome responsibilities that she had felt. And he had certainly never shown an interest in their father's vast empire. Louisiana had been the responsible one, the one who felt a debt had to be paid, the one who knew that she had to justify her relationship to one of the richest and most powerful men in the capitalist world.

She didn't always understand her brother, but, yes, she envied the freedom he had known.

The sun was quickly obliterated by the formation of new rain clouds, casting their shadowy presence over the spired temple. Even at this morning hour, the air was hot and sticky. More rains, she sensed, would come today.

Louisiana loosened the top button of her blouse and closed her eyes, feeling the contrast between this wet, sticky place and the dry, windswept heat of her west-Texas ranch. There, the slightest hint of shade brought relief from the sun. Here, there was no relief.

Oh, Ham! she thought despairingly. *What is going on in your life? I feel like such an outsider here!*

She glanced back through the sliding doors into her suite. The living room held two plush couches covered in a striped green-and-red Thai silk. The furnishings were rich teak with intricate carvings of snakes and winged creatures with godlike heads, the room an exotic blend of luxurious and mysterious.

A sigh escaped her lips. This sense of suspension was not like her. She did not hang in limbo. She was a woman of action, of purpose. There were always a jillion things to do, always plans to set in motion. Life was never static. And while her daddy might have snatched a glance across the river at the temple and uttered, "Now ain't that a purdy sight, daughter?" he would never have wasted precious minutes doing nothing but gawking at it.

Guilt forced Louisiana from her chair. It was absolutely crazy for her to have come all this way and then just do nothing. If Gunner wasn't going to help her, she'd just have to do it on her own. The first thing she would do is go back to Ham's office and demand some answers. She was tired of speculation. She wanted something concrete.

She walked back into the room, sat down at the large teak desk, picked up the phone and placed a call with the overseas operator. Even while away from the office, the chief executive officer of Bond Enterprises had her finger on the pulse. *No, Mrs. Kruger, I'm not coming home just yet.* She listened to the list of crises that had to be resolved ASAP. "You'll handle things just fine," said Louisiana, having no doubts that Mrs. Kruger would. "I'll check with you later about the oil run. You say you should have it in about an hour?"

After hearing the reply she wanted, she hung up without saying goodbye. But then, Mrs. Kruger hadn't expected one.

WHEN IT STRUCK Louisiana full force that this was not a city for a leisurely stroll, it was too late to turn back to the hotel for a taxi. Her blouse clung to her skin like clammy fingers. The broken, uneven sidewalk meant that she had to keep her eyes downward, and even then she was unable to avoid those places where hot, sticky, slow floodwaters lapped at her ankles, drowning her leather shoes. She was sorry now that she had not worn the safari boots, but she had wanted to appear businesslike when she visited Ham's office for the second time. So this morning she had donned her power suit and low sensible pumps.

She had hired a taxi to Ham's office yesterday and the way had not seemed so far. But walking it now along schizoid streets that changed names every two or three blocks, she wondered if she'd ever find it. Like an open-faced sandwich, the sidewalks were spread with a thick slice of humanity. Businessmen slurped noodles from small bowls. Incense smoldered from shrines in front of idle shops. Louisiana passed humble vendors who, colonizing a portion of the sidewalk, cooked chicken in a pungent curry sauce. The spice penetrated her pores until she, too, felt like a stewed hen.

What was it about this place that had so attracted Ham? He had often alluded to its beauty and enchantment, but for the life of her she just couldn't see it. She was used to a canvas of blue-gray skies, warm, dry breezes and lots of room to move around. Open spaces, that was what she needed. She didn't want to be hemmed in. And that was exactly the way she felt here. It was suffocating and stifling, and the endless cacophony from the out-of-sync cars and buses and motorcycles was driving her nuts.

It was just after she saw a snake slithering across the flooded sidewalk in front of her that she sensed an unfriendly presence behind her. There had been so many people around her, and her attention had been so focused on finding her way to Ham's office, that she hadn't noticed the man following her. But when she spotted the snake, she jumped back with the quick reflex of one who had grown up amid the ubiquitous rattlers, cottonmouths and copperheads of west Texas. If she'd had her boots on, she would have stomped it, but it was a species she didn't know and with her designer pumps and bare ankles she wisely chose to let it slide on its way. But as she turned, she saw him—an Oriental man, shorter than she and stocky. His straight black hair was pulled back into a ponytail at the base of his neck, his head partially covered with a brown cap.

Louisiana continued on her way, but she knew the man was behind her. In that brief moment when their eyes had made contact, she sensed that he had been watching her for some time. Why was she being followed?

She picked up the pace of her stride. She wasn't afraid. Louisiana Bond had never been afraid of anyone in her life. As a kid she had wandered alone at night and slept beneath the stars in nothing but a sleeping bag. She and Ham had felt unrestricted and safe upon their father's homestead. They had mingled in complete safety with all the cowhands and the drilling operators. She had been free to run and cavort. And while Ham had been older and too sophisticated for much childish nonsense, Louisiana was always happiest when she'd gallop her horse across the fields, chasing bulls and running meat off the cattle.

She would climb on rig equipment and ride on the shoulders of her father's employees. Once, when she was very young, there had been a kidnap threat against Billy Bond's children, but Louisiana didn't learn of it until many years later. In her mind, childhood had been a safe place to be.

She couldn't imagine why anyone would want to follow her now. The only people who knew she was here were Ham's employees, Duck Tyger and some of those drunks from the bar who wouldn't remember her, anyway.

And Gunner. He knew she was here. And he had advised her to go home.

She had told him about Ham's message. He knew something about his disappearance. And now...there was someone following her.

She turned left onto Sukhumvit Road and darted through the honking traffic. She halted in front of a small shrine and glanced back. The man dashed between cars, still following.

This time she was going to take no chances. She pushed her way through the crowd and hurried the block and a half to Ham's office. Once she got there she would be safe. She would have plenty of people around her who would provide a barrier between herself and whoever was following her.

Crossing another street, she ended up on Krun Eight. The street was narrow and crowded, but she knew she was almost to the office. And because she had practically jogged the last block, she was sure she had lost the man. Wedged between the office of a doctor of numerology and a small gallery of contemporary Thai art, the office of Bond Publications was housed behind an unassuming door with a sign that

read Krung Thep Center. Next to the name was a list
of its offices.

But that was odd. Since she had been here yester-·
day, someone had removed Bond Publications from
the list. All that was left was a sticky impression where
the letters had been. Louisiana glanced back, but the
man was nowhere in sight. She pushed open the door
to the building and climbed the stairs. Her footsteps
made a hollow sound on the steps.

Walking down the hallway to his office, she felt
disoriented, as if she had made a mistake and entered
the wrong building. The offices to her left and right
were the ones she had passed yesterday, but no one was
working today. The building was empty, the unfamiliar silence out of place.

The door to Bond Publications was ajar. Louisiana
stepped through the opening, bewildered by the emp-
tiness that met her. There was nothing here. No desks,
no chairs, no file cabinets. No people. She looked at
the door. The sign for Bond Publications was still
there, but that was all. A cold chill slid up the back of
her neck and goose bumps covered her arms. Where
was everybody? Where had they gone? And why was
the entire building empty?

At that thought, she caught the unmistakable sound
of footsteps. It was the tap of hard-soled shoes climbing the stairs. She froze, every nerve tip in her body
strained to the sound.

The footsteps drew closer, now moving down the
hallway. She grew sick to her stomach.

She glanced around, searching for a place to hide,
but there was nothing to hide behind. There was only
empty, silent space. Ham's private office was just be-

yond and the door to it was open, revealing the
stripped room.

Moving quickly, but as quietly as possible, she tiptoed toward her brother's office. Darting behind the
door, she pressed her back against the wall. She listened, but she heard only the sound of her own
breathing, was aware only of a steady pounding inside her chest. She laid her hand against her heart.

The next sound she heard was footsteps as they entered the outer office. The door closed and the bolt of
the lock slid into place.

She was trapped. She held her breath. Her heart
pounded. Forcing herself to move, she leaned over just
enough to peer through the crack between the door
and the jamb, trying to get a look at the intruder. The
light switch was flipped on and an eerie shadow
stretched across the wall. It was a distorted shape of a
man. A man with hair tied back at the nape of the
neck! The shadow lengthened and her eyes followed
the line of his arm. In his hand was a knife, gro-
tesquely silhouetted against the wall of the outer office. Each footfall beat against her brain like a
hammer on stone. He was drawing close, so close, and
she didn't know what to do. She didn't know which
way to turn. She had never been faced with this kind
of terror. She had known and conquered many an ad-
versary, but none like this. None with knives. His foot
crossed the threshold into Ham's private office.
Louisiana sucked in her breath and a small sound escaped. She watched the man turn, the smile of a vic-
tor upon his face. She pressed back, as if she could
squeeze herself into the wall, as if by sheer force of will
she could be sucked into the plaster and wood. The
knife was no longer in shadow and, through the slim

crack, she saw that the blade was clean and shiny. Brand-new. She wanted to scream, but she couldn't find the voice to do it. He grinned and the hand holding the knife raised ever so slowly.

An explosion rocked her brain. The man turned, startled. The door to the outer office banged open and a man flew into the room, charging like a bull at the one with the knife.

Louisiana clung to the wall and stared out through the slim opening as body flung against body and fist crunched against bone. They tumbled and rolled and pummeled until she could not see where one man began and the other ended.

The knife pinged against the floor and skidded across the room where it hit the baseboard. She thought of going to retrieve it, but she was stuck to the wall with fear.

She heard nothing but groans and grunts coming from deep within the men's chests. They became one, parted, and then, with new blows, became one again.

The battle raged only a matter of minutes, but it felt as if it lasted for hours. The room fell silent. There was only the heavy sound of a man's breath. A body lay inert on the floor—the body of the man who had followed her.

She shook violently as she stood, indecisive, wondering whether she should remain hidden. The choice was taken out of her hands when the door swung around, exposing her to the one who had triumphed over the man on the floor.

She stared, unable to scream or speak or run. This man was nothing like the one who had followed her. This man was huge. And dark. Not delicate like Thai men. And his face was without a single redeeming feature to save it from grim repugnance. She had never seen anyone so formidable. His eyes bore into her. She saw anger and menace and . . . and hate.

A soft whimper escaped her lips. He loosened the red bandanna from around his throat and dabbed it at the cut above his lip. He stuffed it into his breast pocket, then he reached for Louisiana.

She edged to the side, dodging the grip of his hand. But he was faster than she. And stronger.

"Quiet!" he commanded and grabbed for her again. This time he captured her arm.

"No!" She struggled, but his grip was like iron.

He grabbed her purse from the floor. "Come," he growled, hauling her across the room and toward the outer door.

She threw a punch, hoping to catch him off guard. He merely grasped her wrist with one hand and her waist with the other. Then, lifting her like a duffel bag, he tossed her over his shoulder.

He walked quickly now, ignoring the one free hand she used to slap and gouge at his back and neck.

"Let go of me, dammit!"

Her torso bounced against his shoulder as he carried her down the stairs. He didn't loosen his hold a bit.

Out on the sidewalk, she knew she would be able to find help. Someone would hear her yell. Someone would see the way this evil man was treating her. Someone would surely help!

When they reached the sidewalk, she started to scream. Sensing the effort, the man wrapped his arm around her waist, squeezing her until no sound could possibly escape. She tried to find her breath, but he had cut that off, as well. Her vision blurred. Panic filled her. She knew she was going to faint.

Raindrops fell against her face as the man dropped her from his shoulder, swung her around and forced her onto the back of a motorbike. Regaining her breath, she tried to squirm loose, but he forced her again to sit.

"Don't move!" he growled, clutching her wrist in his iron grip. "Hold—here."

Before she could make another attempt to escape, he climbed in front of her, started the engine and drove out into traffic. She grabbed hold of him. The curtain of rain around her kept her disoriented, unaware of how far and fast they were traveling and in which direction they were moving.

He swerved and careered through traffic, and she could do nothing but hang on for dear life. She considered flinging herself off the back of the bike, but only for a brief instant. It would be suicidal. There were hundreds of cars all around them. There was hard concrete and wet filth beneath them. So she clung to his waist and pressed her face against the back of his shirt, protecting her eyes from the rain and the splattering mud.

The bike bounced and jolted her when he drove it onto sidewalks to circle around clogged traffic. Muddy water sprayed up and over them both. Because she was unable to determine where they were, Louisiana kept her face hidden. Time ceased to exist. She was aware only of the bumps and dips, the drenching rain, the hot wind flowing over and around her and the smell of mildew on the man's shirt.

When he finally slowed the bike, she looked up. He veered onto a narrow road that twisted and wound like

the coil of a snake. A thick leafy cover of trees held up
the rain as the bike continued to twist and turn
through a warren of tiny lanes. On each side were rows
of stick houses on stilts, all attached to one another.
They reminded Louisiana of the matchstick houses she
and Ham used to build as children. Hers never lasted.
They always blew down as soon as they were built.
With one good breath of wind, she surmised, these
houses would do the same.

As she rode past them, Louisiana saw that the
houses afforded no privacy. Women sat on the floor
tending children. Old men swept wooden porches or
leaned on crooked canes, visiting with one another. In
front of each house was a small shrine, painted in
brilliant reds and golds and greens.

She smelled stagnant water and saw, at the end of
the lane, a canal. It was one of many on which Bangkok was built.

Just when she thought the man would drive into the
water, plunging them both into its filthy depths, he
made a sharp right turn. She held on.

This lane was even shadier than the ones before, the
huge leaves from the trees weighted down with moisture and drooping over the narrow road. Through the
leaves, and to her left, sampans clustered together in
the canal, floating slowly side by side. Women and
men hollered back and forth from boat to boat, ar-
guing, bartering, exchanging wares.

The man pulled the bike over to the edge of the lane.
He stopped beneath a shady palm in front of a ter-
raced teak house. When he started to climb off,
Louisiana realized her fingers were still gripping his
waist, and it was an effort to pry them loose. She sat
still, wet and hot and miserably lost, wondering if she

would stand a chance of finding her way out of this maze. She had no idea where she was.

The man climbed off the bike and stared at her with sullen hostility. She glared back at him, hating him.

He grasped her arm, which she took as a sign to get off the bike. She climbed off and her knees buckled. His huge hand circled her upper arm and kept her from falling. She felt weak and dizzy, without strength to fight him.

"Come." He pulled her along, half dragging her up some steep wooden steps onto a bare wood porch.

"Where are we?" she managed, but her voice sounded unnaturally low and tired.

"Come. In here." He pulled her through the open doorway, and he sidestepped around her into the small foyer.

She stayed in the doorway, feeling safer near an escape. The man called out something in Thai and Louisiana caught a glimpse of a young woman darting through a room beyond. Louisiana looked around, trying to get some sense of bearing. The house was more sturdily built than it had appeared from the street. It had inward-sloping walls and a steep roof, and she could feel the flow of cool air circulating through its open spaces. Ceiling fans turned slowly, stirring the air.

Her eyes came back to her captor, and she saw that he was still staring at her. But his look now was wary, and his mouth moved as if he wanted to say something but couldn't find the words.

"Bruno?"

Half in shock, she spun toward the new sound to her left. Her mouth fell open when she saw him. She should have known. Dammit, she should have known!

A damsel with a dulcimer
In a vision once I saw

Chapter Five

"You!" she sputtered feebly. "I should have known."
She was too shocked to know if what she felt on see-
ing him was relief or anger. He stood there, his clothes
casual but neat and pressed. In one hand was a news-
paper and in the other a tall glass filled with ice and
liquid. Behind him and a little to the side was the
woman Louisiana had seen darting through the far
room.

Scowling, Gunner took note of Louisiana's
drenched clothes and hair, then turned to Bruno.
"Where did you find her?"

Bruno was still looking at her, dislike and also
something akin to fear in his eyes. The young woman
was looking at her in the same way. "Bond's office,"
he said with a heavy accent and a look of disgust.

The fog in her brain was starting to clear and she
didn't at all like the dark looks that were cast her way.
They were all looking at her as if she were something
slimy that had slithered up from the banks of the
klongs and invaded their inner sanctum.

Bruno, she noticed, glanced at Gunner with a kind
of appeal in his eyes.

Louisiana felt like an exhibit in a zoo. Since she realized the man was in some way associated with Gun-

ner, she had lost her fear of him. Anger was the dominant emotion at play now. "Tell them to stop staring at me," she demanded of Gunner.

Gunner glanced over her head through the opening behind her. "You are standing in the doorway."

She glanced at Bruno, at the girl and then back at Gunner. Her nerves were at their frazzled end. "That," she snapped, "is because I am fixing to leave."

"You're preventing the spirit of the house from getting in or out."

"What?"

"By blocking the doorway. It makes them nervous."

She looked again at the ugly man who had dragged her halfway across the city, through the rain, to this stick house in the depths of some hellish jungle. She looked at the girl, edging closer to Gunner as if he were a shield. "That is the dumbest thing I have ever—"

"Please," Gunner said.

"Oh, for Pete's sake." Louisiana sighed, stepping out of the doorway. "Now is everyone happy?"

No one answered. Gunner and Bruno were looking at each other and Bruno was speaking in his strong Oriental accent. "One of Tak's men followed her." The downturn of his mouth indicated the fact that she was followed was entirely her fault.

Her body began to shake as the memory of the man with the knife came back. This big hulk standing here had probably saved her life, but he hadn't even bothered to explain that. And now he acted as if he had made a big mistake in doing so.

And Gunner, what did he have to do with this? What the hell was going on!

She saw that Gunner was looking at her. His mouth was tight, his eyes narrowed on her. "Well, were you hurt?"

She stared back at him, as all the terror and pain came flooding back. She began to shake. All over. Her knees felt as if they had turned to jelly and were going to buckle beneath her. The room swam before her eyes. "Hurt?" she gritted through clenched teeth. She glanced at Bruno, then back at Gunner, forcing herself to step toward him. Her fist raised. "You stinkin' son of a—"

Gunner reached up and grasped her wrist before her hand made contact with his face. It was held viselike in his grip. "Listen, darlin'," he said with a thick mockery of her accent, "before you display your whole repertoire of Texas cusswords, I suggest you collect yourself. You look like something the cat dragged in."

"Don't you mean something your ape dragged in?" she snarled.

He chuckled and translated the word in Thai to the other man. Bruno didn't laugh.

Gunner's eyes fastened on her face, his voice and emotions tightly controlled. "Why don't you get cleaned up. You'll feel better."

Her fist remained clenched, her mouth squeezed shut. But Gunner didn't let go. They stood this way, glaring at each other for an endless moment, she with the force of her anger centered in her closed fist and in her pinched face, and he with his dominance and stubborn will centered in his eyes and in the grasp of her arm.

She surrendered first, too depleted to fight anymore. She didn't understand any of this. She was still suffering from jet lag. She was hot and wet and lost. She was blocking spirits from the damn doorway. She was in a room with people who spoke an incomprehensible language. She was confronting a man who had been a ruthless mercenary and who now knew something about her brother's disappearance. She hated them all. She hated this place. She wanted to go home. Unfortunately they seemed to be the key to finding out what had happened to her brother. They had the answers she sought.

Her fist relaxed and Gunner lowered her arm to her side. His smile suggested that he'd known all along she would surrender. He nodded toward the young woman behind him. "Soon-Ni will fix a cool bath for you."

Louisiana glanced at the girl's wary, distrustful eyes, then she looked back at Gunner. "I don't want a bath. I want to know what is going on. Why am I here? Tell me."

Gunner turned to Soon-Ni and said something in Thai, then he looked back at Louisiana. "I will. I promise."

With reluctance but without the strength to argue further, Louisiana allowed herself to be led away by the girl. She followed her through an open, breeze-filled living room and on into the bedroom beyond. Soon-Ni gave Louisiana no time to linger or look around her, but led her directly into a large bathroom.

The room, as the rest of the house, was built entirely of teak. The walls, the round tub and the counter were all made of the same durable yellow-brown wood. A high round window overlooked the rice barges and sampans that drifted lazily down the rain-misted *klong*.

Soon-Ni filled the tub and poured something that smelled of jasmine into the water. She laid out a huge thick green towel and washcloth, then turned to Louisiana. "You want wash?"

Louisiana stared at her. She couldn't have been more than sixteen. She was small and shy and did not want to look at Louisiana but for brief seconds at a time.

"No, I can do that."

The girl turned to leave.

"Thank you," said Louisiana, but the girl quietly slipped out of the room through the curtained doorway.

Louisiana turned to the mirror over the sink and stared at her mud-streaked face. How pathetic she looked! Pathetic and lost. She had never been lost in her life. She had always had a strong sense of direction. She was goal oriented. She knew where she was and where she was heading at all times. Yet here she was, wet and pitiful and standing in the middle of a stranger's bathroom.

How safe was she here? There were two men in this house who obviously disliked her. One she knew had been a paid killer; the other had killed a man this morning and had kidnapped a woman this afternoon. Her. She had been kidnapped! Shanghaied! No, she was anything but safe in this house. Still—

The aroma of jasmine and the clear tubful of water beckoned her. Slowly she peeled off her blouse and skirt, discarding her mud-soaked clothes in a pile by the door. She wondered where her purse was. The ape, she decided, must have given it to Gunner. She stepped into the cool water and sank down.

The intoxicating scent that lifted from the cool water filled her mind with peace. She leaned her head back against the rim of the tub and closed her eyes.

An image of a handsome, tanned face swam before her eyes. She thought of the way he had looked last night at the bar and then at the hotel. She thought of the way he'd looked a moment ago. Even while exuding danger and still holding a tight rein of control, there was a relaxed air about him. It was the way he dressed, the way he stood, the way his voice, so deep and commanding, spoke only of what was essential, wasting no words. And it was his eyes, eyes that had seen much but that told little.

She sank down under the water, wetting her hair. There was a bottle sitting on the rim of the tub, but the print was in Thai. She unscrewed the lid and held the bottle beneath her nose. It smelled wonderful. She poured a little into the palm of her hand and rubbed it into a lather. She massaged it into her hair, scrubbing away the mud that was caked against her scalp.

As she sank down once again beneath the water, she wondered vaguely if there had been other women who had stepped out of Gunner's bathroom, smelling of jasmine and exotic herbs.

Several minutes later, she climbed out of the tub and wrapped the big soft towel around her. She glanced over toward the curtain and saw that her dirty pile of clothes had been replaced with some clean ones. She walked over and picked up a man-size shirt and a pair of pants with a drawstring waist.

She dressed, feeling refreshed and whole again. She knew that she now had the strength to face the man with the answers. She had come halfway around the world for them and she would not be put off any longer.

She draped the towel over the back of a rattan chair and pushed aside the curtain in the doorway. She stopped in the middle of Gunner's bedroom, studying the room around her. For coolness' sake the window openings were shuttered, but through the green slats she could see the canal and the rice fields beyond. Tiny drops of rain drizzled down against the shutters, blurring the view.

The bed was large and covered with a colorful textile spread. The furnishings were spare, but on every surface were stacks of books. She ran her eyes down the stack. Nietzsche's *Beyond Good and Evil,* Bacon's *Essays,* Churchill, Emerson, Cicero. Moving to the other side of the room, she looked at another stack. It was more of the same. Mostly philosophy. On the walls were photographs of Thailand. Some were of little brown children, naked except for big straw hats, bathing in a canal. There was one of an old woman sitting under a faded yellow umbrella, weaving a piece of cloth that looked like the one draped over his bed. There was one of a beautiful young Thai girl carving vegetables into exquisite flower shapes. There were photographs of scenery, places that were mist filled and mystical, scenes displaced from time itself. But all of the pictures showed one thing—a love and a deep respect for the country.

She replaced the books and walked out of the bedroom and into the living room. These walls, too, were covered with pictures depicting Thai life, many of children expressing inexplicable glee in the midst of their poverty.

The room had no outer wall. It was open to a veranda just beyond the room. She saw Gunner standing at the railing, his hands resting on the top rail, his back to the house. Her purse was on a nearby table.

She stepped through the opening, feeling a breeze from the thick covering of trees around the terrace. She looked up. The veranda was covered with bamboo and vines, and not a drop of rain penetrated its veil.

He turned and his eyes made a slow appraisal of what he saw. She had looked great last night, but she looked even better now, wearing his clothes. Soft and accessible.

"Do you have a phone?" she asked.

Well, he thought, *so much for accessible.* "Yeah. Right there."

"Can I get an overseas operator from here?"

"With luck."

Fighting the desire to relax for a minute and join Gunner at the railing of his porch, Louisiana went to the phone and spent the next fifteen minutes trying to place a call to her office. Once connected, she spent another five minutes going over the oil runs that Mrs. Kruger had finally received.

While she discussed one-eighth interests and shut-in payments over the phone, Gunner watched her. She was all business now, no softness left except in the drawn-out "hons" and "sugars" that ran like molasses between the directives. She was an interesting specimen, that was for sure. One with which he was not entirely comfortable. He had left the States at the emergence of the feminist movement and had lived around women with old-world values for quite a few years. And while he had always prided himself on

having an open mind and was the first to admit that
potential and intellect had little to do with gender, this
woman's ability to maneuver pawns on the corporate
chessboard was not without its intimidating aspects.

He also had to admit another thing to himself—this
woman intrigued him.

When Louisiana finished her call, she hung up the
phone and sighed wearily. There had been a time when
every aspect of the business had stimulated her. When
Daddy Bond was alive, she had stood beside him,
breathing the same invigorating scent of assets and
procurements and capital returns. Those had been the
good old boom days when no Texas oilman could
possibly lose.

But things were different now. The minerals of the
earth had become bargaining chips in a global con-
ference, the rattling saber of ever-increasing threats.
The fun just wasn't there anymore. Maybe it was because her daddy was gone. Maybe it was because there
was just too much weight for her shoulders to bear
alone. Or maybe it was simply because she was standing here feeling envy for a man who looked perfectly
at ease and in tune with this slow, languorous world.

She stepped onto the veranda and walked over to the
railing beside Gunner. She had been so busy with her
phone call, she hadn't noticed the scene beyond this
deck. Now it caught her by surprise.

The house was turned sideways, the canal running
along at an angle. The view before her was of a floating flower market to the right, a thick, leafy glade of
fruit and palm trees behind the veranda and, to the
left, a beautiful garden complete with flowers, more
fruit trees and tropical birds splashing in a tiny pool of
clear water.

But it was the canal that held her attention. It was so dark and muddy, its depth concealed from her. People bathed in it and drank from it. They fished and traded goods from their sampans. The canals—these dirty, foul-smelling rivers of sludge—were the very foundation of life for the Thai people.

"You look frightened."

Louisiana jerked, startled out of her disquieting thoughts. As she tried to see beyond the closed wall of his expression, she realized that the water and the pace of life here were not the only things that troubled her. This man disturbed her very much. He made her feel things she had no time or inclination to feel.

"Frightened?" She smirked, hoping to offset the power he had over her. "I was followed by a stranger through the flooded streets of this city. There is no sign of life at my brother's office." Her voice grew more shrill. "A man came at me with a knife. This—this—person of yours kidnapped me, threw me over his shoulder and carted me off to God-only-knows-where-I-am on his motorcycle." She glared at him. "Frightened, Gunner? I can't imagine why you'd say that."

"That's not what I meant." He continued to regard her with little emotion. "I meant this place. You look frightened by—by all of this."

She glanced around, but her gaze skipped over the canal. "That's ridiculous, darlin'. *Places* don't frighten a Bond."

"Ah, yes, I almost forgot. The well-heeled, intrepid world travelers. William B. Bond and his plucky daughter."

Her mouth tightened and she crossed her arms. "I *have* been a few places."

"Paris?" He smiled. "Milano? Oh, and of course the Via Condotti in Rome."

She wasn't going to let him get to her. She could hold her own against anyone in the corporate world. Some retired tin soldier was no match at all. She refused to admit that the man standing before her emitted a scent of power and command unlike any she had ever encountered. "I have also been to places like Quito. Khartoum. Cairo."

He leaned back against the railing and crossed his arms, his mouth slanted sideways in a half smile. "What about Asia?"

"What about it?" she snapped.

He spoke as if to a child, infuriating her even more. "Have you ever been to Asia before?"

Her fingers drummed on the top of the railing as she looked for traps. "Hong Kong."

He smiled. "Of course."

"What is that supposed to mean?"

He shrugged. "I'm sure like most Westerners, you assume that Hong Kong is the quintessential Asia."

Louisiana cocked her head, invoking her own patronizing tone. "I take it you're talking about something other than geography."

He turned around, once again resting his arms on the railing, his eyes focused on the glade beyond. Through the branches, rice fields could be seen stretching to the horizon.

When he didn't answer, she said, "Bangkok. I've now been to Bangkok. This is Asia."

His eyes narrowed, his gaze reaching to those far paddies beyond. "It used to be."

As quickly as the confrontation had begun, it had dissipated. But somehow Louisiana didn't feel as if she had won any battle. It was more as if a plug had been pulled, letting the animosity drip away like a slow leak. She wanted to keep the irritation in her voice, but her strength was gone.

"What changed it?"

He looked over at her and gave a slight shrug. "Vietnam, for starters."

God, but he made her tired! What was it about him that did this to her? Was it the verbal sparring or was it that just to look at him made her feel things that depleted her store of energy? She should walk away. She should go to the police and have them help her find out what had happened to her brother. And yet Ham had written to her about this man. He had told her to seek him out. There had to be a reason for that. "In what way did it do that?" she asked.

"Oh, you know, the influx of Westerners, of the military, of foreign capital."

"You're saying the Thai economy hasn't been improved by American and European capital?"

He glanced her way. "People have become wealthy over it, I'll give you that. But..." The thought hung as they watched a family float by on their sampan. "Improved?" He shook his head.

Louisiana had grown up with the power of money always at hand. It could change lives, that she knew. But the rationale of her kind was that it was always for the better. Money—especially American dollars—improved the world.

"You were one of the soldiers," she retaliated. "You and Ham contributed to the changes here, didn't you?"

"Yes."

"And you didn't stop with Vietnam. You tipped the scales in other places, as well."

If she had expected Gunner to flinch under the accusation, she was disappointed. He merely said, "Something we were paid to do."

She cleared her throat. "So—where's your henchman?"

"Bruno?"

"Such a fitting name."

"His name is really Sol Heu."

"He doesn't look Thai."

"He's not. His mother was half French, half Cambodian. His father was Chinese."

"So what is he, your bodyguard or something?"

Gunner smiled. "My friend."

"Does he shanghai ladies for you whenever you ask?"

"I don't remember asking for you."

Louisiana's lips tightened at the verbal slap. "So how did he know I was there?"

Gunner leaned sideways against the railing, his arms crossed, and studied her. "He was following you."

"Why?"

"Since you waltzed into the Tiger Den last night, you're obviously not the type who's afraid of barging in where you don't belong."

"Are you saying, darlin', that I don't belong at my brother's office?"

"I think you already found the answer to that question."

She frowned as the frightening memory came back to her. "Where did everyone go? Yesterday the building was filled with people. Today no one was there.

And Ham's office was totally empty. Not a piece of furniture. Not a file. Nothing.''

He shrugged, unconcerned. "Someone obviously wanted the building cleared."

"But who?"

"Money wields power in this part of the world, too."

"But, Gunner, why would someone want to do that? And why would someone want to—to hurt me?"

Gunner was silent for a long moment while he stared at her. "To kill you, Louisiana," he finally said. "Not to hurt you. To kill you."

The blood drained to her feet. "Why?" she asked more softly. "What the hell kind of trouble is Ham in?"

He was too quiet. The sounds of birds chattering in the trees around them filled the thick, hot air. Her breathing stopped and her voice was unusually quiet. "It was you, wasn't it?" she said in wonder. "It wasn't Ham at all. Someone was after me because I was talking to you."

His eyes grew dark and veiled. "It's possible."

She regarded him for a long moment, slipping this new piece into the intricate puzzle. "Why? Who—who are you, Gunner?"

The inscrutable mask dropped into place once more. "I said it was possible, that's all."

"You have enemies?"

"Don't be naive, Louisiana."

"I'm trying to be thorough. I'm trying to understand what is going on here! Are you and Ham involved in something together?"

Soon-Ni came up behind them and set a tray of drinks and sandwiches on the table. She hastily left the terrace, and as Louisiana's gaze followed her, she saw the girl go to a straw mat inside the house and sit down on it.

"Why is she on the floor?"

Gunner followed her line of vision. "That's where she sits."

"She's not allowed in a chair?"

He gave Louisiana a long look of appraisal. "Don't come in here with your Westernized ways and expect to change Thai people...Thai women. She's not American."

Louisiana glanced at the girl and then at Gunner. She cocked her head and a knowing smirk played around her lips. "What is she, sixteen? Seventeen?"

"If you're about to pass some sort of moral judgment, and jump to the absurd conclusion that she's my concubine or some such, I suggest you don't."

"Oh, that's right," she said smugly. "This is Thailand. This isn't America."

Gunner reached for a glass on the table and handed it to her. He grabbed a sandwich and smiled. "Eat something and drink your juice, Louisiana."

She looked at the pulpy liquid in the glass.

"Of course, if I'd known you were going to drop by for a visit," he said, "I would have stocked up on Yukon Jack."

"What is this?"

"Som-O. Pomelo. Try it. It's a fruit made in heaven."

"Right." She took a gingerly sip, expecting the worst, but not about to let him know it. She was pleasantly surprised when the sweet fruity liquid soothed her throat as it went down.

"Like it?"

She nodded, not wanting to lay out any undue praise as yet.

"So is that what you do all day back in Texas?"

"What's that?"

He cocked his head toward the phone. "All that industrious, capitalistic stuff."

"Well, sugar, I don't sit home and crochet."

"What about charity work? I thought that's what all those other rich women did back in the States."

"Charity! Gracious sakes alive! Daddy would come back to haunt me."

"What, he didn't believe in it?"

"Not unless the Aggies were having a bad year."

Gunner chuckled. "Funny, I never thought of football as a charity."

"Well, to Daddy it was a holy shrine."

"You know," he said, studying her, "I thought you would get a taste of the danger over here and then scurry back to the States as fast as you could. I misjudged you."

"Seems you did. It also seems that you have misjudged my relationship with my brother. We're family. And we are very close."

Gunner sighed. "Look, Louisiana, you have to understand that there's a right way and a wrong way to find somebody. You can't just go plowing through the world like it's one big Texas cornfield or—or cotton field or whatever kind of fields you have down there."

"Oil fields."

"Right. Oil fields. Life is different here. There's a pace that must be followed. *Jai yen,* Louisiana."

"What's that?"

"A cool heart. It's a trait practiced in this part of the world. Much admired." He studied her closely.

"You know, things here are not always what they seem. People aren't, either."

Louisiana ate part of a sandwich and finished her juice. She set the glass on the table and looked out over the lush tropical garden that flourished beside his house. Other than the beautiful gardens at the hotel, she had seen little of Thailand's enchantment. She had been harassed, and rained on, and driven down one dead end after another. But this, this one small garden said quite a bit about the place and the people who lived here.

"Yes, I see you have some surprises, too."

"You mean all this?" He waved his arm over the garden. "Why shucks, ma'am, that ain't nothin'."

She smiled. "It's beautiful."

He shrugged. "The place lends itself to that."

"Yeah? I hadn't really noticed. I've been kind of busy with noticing the rain, and mud, and ill-bred drunken yahoos. I think I've caught a glimpse of a gaudy temple or two." She paused, thinking. "You know—all this asceticism . . . Ham has been writing to me about Buddhism, but I find it hard to believe that he would be drawn to it."

"It offers a kind of peace."

"Are you a Buddhist?"

Gunner shook his head. "No. I gave up looking for answers a long time ago."

Louisiana sighed. "Ham has always been searching for something. I miss him so much sometimes. For a while I thought he might come back to Texas and help me run the company. But—" she shook her head "—he seems to have built a life here." She glanced out over the water, her eyes reflecting all the bewilderment she felt.

Gunner watched her closely. "Don't be deceived by Thailand's surface, Louisiana. Behind the facade, paradise awaits."

Her eyes locked with his. "I didn't come in search of paradise, Gunner."

His voice was low and openly seductive. "Maybe you could use a little."

Some long-hidden desire snaked just beneath her skin, but she briskly rubbed her hands along her arms in an attempt to make the sensation go away. "I came here to find my brother. You know something about his disappearance, Gunner. You know that he's in some kind of danger, don't you?"

Gunner stared into that incredibly soft but determined face and felt himself sliding into a trap of his own making. Bruno was right. The woman spelled trouble, but he didn't know what he was going to do about her.

"This is not a corporate boardroom, Louisiana. Civilized rules simply don't apply."

"I'm not afraid."

"You should be."

"Will you help me?"

This could mess you up for a long time, he warned himself. Come on, you know how to avoid this kind of thing. You're a master at it. You've never been a sucker for a silken voice. But dammit! Just to look at those intense green eyes...

"I have to find him, Gunner. He's all the family I have."

Gunner felt the net close over him and he cursed inwardly. There was a way out of this. There had to be. But as he thought about it, he realized that the long years of virulent warfare had failed to teach him one very basic skill for survival—how to avoid the lure of a damsel in distress. Even one who could, without much effort, drop her net over his whole operation and ruin everything.

Voices inside the house filtered out to them and Louisiana recognized Bruno's. He came out to the veranda, his face creased in tension. Gunner, alerted to a new current in the air, stepped away from the railing.

"What is it?"

Bruno answered him in Thai.

"What did he say?" asked Louisiana.

After a moment's hesitation, Gunner said, "Your brother's apartment has been ransacked."

"Ham's?" she exclaimed, out of shock.

Bruno said something else and Gunner listened with rapt attention. "Damn, two of them you say?"

Bruno nodded.

"What!" demanded Louisiana. "What!"

"There are a couple of guys waiting on Luang Song."

"Where's that?"

"An office I occasionally use." He looked back at Bruno. "You talked to the monk?"

Bruno nodded. "The abbot is gone."

"And the statue?"

"Gone."

"What is he talking about?" demanded Louisiana. "What is all this gobbledygook? Does it have something to do with Ham?"

Gunner and Bruno shared a long calculating stare and then Gunner turned toward Louisiana. His words, when he spoke, were slow and even, each one carefully weighed. "A few weeks ago, Ham found something."

"What do you mean, he found something?"

"You know this thing he has for archeology. The bit in the message he sent you."

"Yes."

"Well, that's what I mean. He found something." Gunner shrugged. "It didn't seem all that spectacular a find at first. It was a Buddha image, just plaster. At least, that was what Ham thought."

"What was so special about it?"

"It wasn't plaster. It had been painted with something that resembled plaster, but Ham found a crack in it."

Louisiana's breath was suspended in the still afternoon air. "What was it?"

Gunner hesitated. "Jade."

The breath left Louisiana in a loud rush. "Real jade?"

Gunner nodded. "The real thing."

Her heart began to beat faster. "Go on."

Gunner glanced around. "There was something else about the Buddha image. It had some sort of carving on the back. Ham was pretty excited about it."

"Why, what did it mean?"

Gunner shook his head. "I don't know, exactly. It had to do with some ancient legend. Truthfully, at the time, I had other things on my mind and I just wasn't all that interested."

"When did he tell you about it?"

"He told me about the jade when he first got back from the dig. But this other thing—this legend—I didn't find that out until a few days ago. You see, he brought the statue back here to the temple. He gave it to Po."

"Who's Po?"

"An abbot at the temple. He is one of the official government scholars. He's also Ham's teacher."

"Teacher of what?"

"Buddhism."

She frowned. "This guy, Po, was teaching Ham how to become a Buddhist?"

"Something like that. They became good friends. Anyway, Ham gave the statue to Po for safekeeping. Apparently it was a very important find."

"Okay, so he brought it back to the abbot. Why would that put Ham in danger?"

"Bruno just found out . . . Po is gone."

"What do you mean, gone?"

"Missing. The statue is missing, also."

"Do you mean to tell me that Ham and the missing abbot and the missing Buddha are all connected?"

She waited for his answer, watching him closely. But when he said, "Very much so, Louisiana," she saw him glance at Bruno. And she felt sure that he was not telling her everything. He and his henchman, Bruno, were holding something back. And she was damn sure going to find out what that something was.

"So what do we do now?" she asked.

Gunner smiled patronizingly. "You're going back to your hotel, that's what." He turned back to Bruno. "Guess I'd better go see Roxy."

"Who's Roxy?" asked Louisiana.

Gunner ignored her as he gave instructions to Bruno. He told him to go back to the house on Luang Song and keep an eye on the men hanging around outside. "See where they go. Louisiana's going back to her hotel."

She snapped her head toward him. "I most certainly am not. I'm going wherever you go."

Gunner's eyes slid over her in quick appraisal. "Honey, you may have fooled Duck Tyger into thinking you belonged at the Den. But you won't fool anybody on Patpong."

Her chin shot forward. "Why? What is Patpong?"

He sniffed derisively. "A place you don't belong."

Her chin shot forward. "You're saying I'm not equipped to handle this—this place, whatever it is?"

Gunner leaned close. His voice was low and hard. "My guess is that it's not equipped to handle you. And I'm saying that you're not going."

Weave a circle round him thrice,
And close your eyes with holy dread

Chapter Six

By the time they got back to Louisiana's hotel, it was almost seven o'clock. At the hotel's front entrance, Gunner grasped both of her arms and turned her to face him. "All this righteous indignation is going to get you nowhere with me, Louisiana. Now I want you to stay here until I come back."

"Who is Roxy, Gunner?"

He hesitated before answering. "She's a friend of your brother's. A good friend, Louisiana."

"Then why shouldn't I go talk to her?"

"You wouldn't understand."

"I am chairman of the board of one of the largest oil companies in America. I understand more than you're willing to admit."

"I want you to stay here, Louisiana. You're to stay in your room and keep the door locked. Don't open it until I come back. You got that?"

She watched him walk away from her and get into a taxi. It pulled away, with him inside, assured that she would obey his every wish and command.

She smiled shrewdly to herself. Well, here was a man who didn't know Louisiana Bond well at all. Nobody told her what to do.

She turned to the boy at the door. "You would like a taxi?" he asked.

"Yes, but quickly."

"Of course."

She shifted from foot to foot while the boy picked up a phone to call another cab. Meanwhile, Gunner was leaving her behind. His taxi had almost reached the end of the block.

A few feet away, she spotted what the locals affectionately called a *tuk-tuk*. More properly known as a *samlor*, the tiny three-wheeled vehicle offered the only chance for catching up with Gunner. A driver dozed in the front seat.

She ran over to him and shook him. "Wake up. Hurry, please."

The startled driver jumped and straightened around as Louisiana climbed into the open-air back and pointed to the taxi up ahead. It was just turning the corner. "Follow that taxi."

He shook the sleep from his head and grinned excitedly at her for a long moment. "Like in American movie!"

"Yes, yes," she cried impatiently. "Please, just hurry!"

The little *tuk-tuk* engine roared and the driver took off down the street. He squealed around the corner, and Louisiana had to grip the side poles to stay in her seat. The wind beneath the open canopy whipped at her face, but the driver never slowed down. Gunner's taxi had moved far ahead of them and she was afraid she was going to lose him.

"He's heading for Patpóng. Do you know it?"

The driver turned to stare at her. "Pa'p'ng?"

"Yes."

His grin grew wider. "I know short way." He applied the brakes and Louisiana was thrown forward in the seat. He turned the *samlor* around and drove in the opposite direction.

"No!" she cried. "I want to go where that taxi goes."

The driver never slowed down. "Pa'p'ng. Yes. I take you there. Short time."

Her heart sank when she saw the mass of congested traffic in front of them, but the undaunted driver pulled the *samlor* up onto the sidewalk and wove in and out of the vendors' stalls as he raced through the clogged intersection. They plunked back down off the sidewalk and into the street, spraying water on unfortunate pedestrians.

Louisiana clung to the poles for support and prayed that this man knew what he was doing. At this point, she had no choice but to hang on for dear life and let him drive.

Amazingly enough, as her driver pulled into a curb and parked, she saw Gunner step out of his taxi.

"Not too close," she whispered, slinking back against the seat. Gunner didn't even notice her. He paid the driver of the cab and strode down a street that was no wider than an alley, its sidelines illuminated by flashing neon signs.

Evening had crept over the city like a thief, robbing Louisiana of any sense of time. The day had slipped from her grasp in less than a moment and yet it also seemed days since she had hidden from her assailant in Ham's office. "This is Patpong?"

The driver grinned and bobbed his head. "Pa'p'ng."

Louisiana looked at the homemade meter hanging from the canvas awning. "Your meter isn't working."

He continued to grin. "No work."

"How much do I owe you?"

"Ahh—" He scribbled the amount on a wrinkled piece of paper.

"Three hundred *baht!* You must be joking!" She quickly calculated how far they had come and compared it with her trip the other day from the airport. Still, he had gotten her here. "I'll give you forty." She handed him the money, still marveling that Bruno and Gunner hadn't robbed her blind while they had the chance with her purse.

He shook his head. "No, lady. No way." He wrote down two hundred.

She handed him twenty more *baht.* "Sixty." She stepped out. He jumped out and followed her down the street.

"No, lady. No, lady."

Gunner was fifty feet ahead of her, but she didn't want the commotion to draw his attention. She reached into her purse and pulled out twenty more *baht.* "This is it!" she said. "No more." She hurried away, and when she turned around she saw the little man grinning and waving at her. "Louisiana," she murmured to herself, "you're such a sap."

She stopped and stared down the short, narrow street that was lined with flashing neon lights and garish posters. Hawkers outside raucous bars proudly touted kinky sex shows and international delights that awaited on the other side of the doors. So this was Patpong. The red-light district. Louisiana didn't have to guess too hard to know exactly what awaited on the other side. Noise, rowdy men, underage and under-dressed Thai girls, and overpriced drinks.

And, she guessed, Roxy.

But why here? She was a friend of Ham's, but what kind of friend? Did she live here? Work here?

She looked up at the names of the bars. Butterfly. Superstar. Pink Panther.

She saw Gunner turn into one called Hot Stuff.

Louisiana took a deep breath and marched in behind him. The barker outside said, "You want massage, lady! Good price."

"I'll pass, thanks."

Inside, the bar was a collage of bright flashing lights and blaring music. A long bar ran down the center of the room, with a platform behind it on which were firemen's poles and lots of mirrors. Scantily clad girls held on to the poles and gyrated to the loud music. Beefy foreign expatriates clapped and whooped their approval.

Louisiana attracted a few curious stares when she walked in, but not too many. One quick look told most of the men in the bar that she was way out of their price range. They had saved up a week's worth of pay working the offshore rigs and jungle seismic crews, and now they were in town for Bangkok's equivalent to the blue plate special.

She sat in the back where she could keep an eye on the smoke-filled room. And on Gunner. He had found a seat at the bar and had already ordered a beer.

A short round man with a bald head walked up to her table. "Sawasdee," he said, bowing with his hands pressed together beneath his nose.

She nodded. "Hello."

"You want drink?"

This must be the manager, she decided. And, like Duck, he probably wondered what the hell she thought she was doing, taking up valuable space in his bar without ordering a drink. "No, thank you. I'm—waiting for someone. Actually," she ventured hopefully, "I'm looking for a girl named Roxy."

"We have many girls. You not like them?"

"No, no, you don't understand. I—she's a friend. Her name is Roxy."

"A friend?"

"Yes."

"Here?"

Louisiana sighed. "Do you have someone who—who works here by the name of Roxy?"

He smiled pleasantly. "No, not here." He smiled again. "You drink. Have good time. We have many girls. Or if you want boy, I can arrange."

"No," she croaked. "I—really, I'm just—maybe I will have a drink. A beer, please."

He smiled and walked away.

Her head was beginning to pound from all the noise and lights, and she wanted nothing more than to find a bed somewhere and crawl into it. So much had happened since last night and it seemed like days since she'd had any sleep.

Her beer came, but she barely touched it. She was watching Gunner. He tipped his bottle and watched the show on the bar above him with detached emotion. There was something about him that set him apart from every other man in the bar. Something quiet and focused. Several young girls came up to him, obviously offering their services. When he declined, they smiled, shrugged and moved on to those more willing to partake.

Louisiana couldn't help but let her thoughts wander to Gunner's personal life. There were the bottles of feminine fragrance sitting on the shelf of his tub, right next to the more masculine ones. She tried not to let the idea of another woman in his life affect her. After all, she hardly knew him. And she certainly didn't trust him. Still . . . she wondered.

It had been a long time since she'd had a relationship with anyone. With so many fiscal and corporate responsibilities, there was very little time in her life for romance. And Daddy Bond hadn't been big on what he referred to as "social meanderin'," so she had never adopted the habit for herself. Of course, Billy had more than his share of intimate relationships in life, but Louisiana had never found it all that easy. A man could go out to a place like this bar and find a date. He could take her home, marry her, whatever he chose. But it wasn't the same for a woman. Most of the men Louisiana knew had no trouble dealing with impermanence. She, on the other hand, had to have more. The big question was, who was the loneliest?

She sipped her watered-down beer and studied Gunner, thinking about what it might have been like had she met him in a different place. Yet somehow she couldn't picture him anywhere else. He was right at home on his veranda, with the sludgy canals crawling by and the tropical birds flitting from one fig tree to another. She tried to picture him in the hot, dry plains of Texas, boots jangling in the dust, but the image was distorted and surreal.

A small, slim girl slipped out from behind a tattered curtain and Gunner started to stand. But when the girl caught a glimpse of Gunner, she ducked behind the curtain and was gone.

He dropped a *baht* note on the bar and was off the stool in a matter of seconds. He wended his way through the crowd and toward the door. Louisiana jumped up and followed him, staying close, but not too close. She wanted to know what was going on here, but she didn't want to do anything that would give Gunner the opportunity to force her away again.

He darted down an alley that cut between a couple of bars. At the end was a stairway leading up to an apartment. Louisiana slipped into the shadows a few feet away and waited, watching him. A scowling giant who looked as if he had been carved from a side of beef planted himself in front of the stairs, blocking Gunner's path. The arms folded across his chest were the size of most men's legs.

"You not go up."

"I've come to see Roxy," said Gunner.

The man shook his head. "No Roxy here."

"Look," said Gunner with more patience than Louisiana could have mustered. "She's a friend."

"Many friends on Patpong."

"Not that kind."

"Only one kind of friend here," he insisted.

Gunner pulled out a green *baht* note and handed it to the man. "I need to talk to her."

The man dropped the money on the ground. "No talk. She not working now."

Gunner stooped down very slowly to pick up the note and Louisiana felt like yelling at him. Don't give up that easily! she wanted to say, but before the words could fully form in her mind, he came up with the speed of light and his elbow slammed into the other man's stomach.

When the guard got his wind back, he came at Gunner with a left drive toward the head.

Gunner sidestepped it, pivoted around and, getting more weight behind it, threw a right hook into the man's solar plexus.

The guard staggered back, doubled over and slid slowly down the wall, one leg crumpling beneath him and the other sticking straight out in front of him. His eyes—in the seconds before he blacked out—were wide with shock.

Louisiana sidled out from her hiding place. "Are you okay? That was great! You're really—"

Gunner spun around. His eyes were wide, his breath hard. Before she could dodge him, he had grasped her arms and shoved her up against the wall. "What the hell are you doing here!"

Her eyes widened in fright. He looked different, charged with electricity, packed with power. "L-let go of me!" she stammered.

His hands gripped her upper arms as he pushed her against the wall. "I asked you a question, dammit. Now answer me!"

She lifted her chin and glared at him, but her heart pounded like an assault of horses' hooves against a paddock door. "I came to talk to her," she managed. "To Roxy."

He didn't loosen the pressure on her, but his eyes, dark and deep, searched her face for truths and lies. "You followed me," he growled. "I told you to stay put."

She stared steadily at him, but her brain felt caught in mid-flight. The flashing lights above formed tantalizing patterns, like those of dancing girls, on the wet pavement beneath their feet. Her words lengthened. "You don't tell me what to do, Gunner."

His voice, too, shifted, the timbre low and unsure. "You shouldn't be here."

Her heart beat against the wall enclosing it as she stared at him. "Why not? You're here."

"Someone tried to kill you today."

The moist heat between them was suffocating her. She wanted to touch him, but he still gripped her arms. Her hands remained flattened against the wall. "Someone has staked out your office, Gunner. You are obviously in as much danger as I am."

"So stay away, Louisiana."

Say my name again, she wanted to tell him. "No," she answered stubbornly.

Like two heat exchangers, the unfamiliar currents of longing bounded between them.

She reminded herself that she needed him only to find her brother.

He reminded himself that she was trouble.

"You'll get hurt," he whispered warningly.

In a small apartment across the alley, a ceiling fan turned slowly, stirring the heat, slinging blurred shadows on the gray wall of the tiny room. "You won't let me," she whispered back.

He leaned into the kiss. She met him halfway.

His mouth came down over hers, warm as the night, as potent as incense. His hands loosened their grip on her arms, and the pressure changed. One hand slid up over her shoulder and onto the side of her neck. His thumb pressed against the base of her jaw, tipping her head back. She felt as if she were falling into a dense forest bed, dragging him down with her. Electricity surged between them. All the energy and heat from his mouth focused in a narrow beam that shot through the core of her body.

His mouth slid to her ear and the sound of his breathing filled her with intense longing. A longing that had to be suppressed.

With maddening restraint, his hand slid down her arm and she was released. She stared into his face, her ragged breath an infuriating sign of weakness. And yet she knew, by the feel of his warm breath against her cheek and the pressure of his lips against hers, that he had felt it, too. The urges had not been hers alone.

"I'm not going to let you foul up my life, Louisiana."

She struggled to find an edge. "I have no intention or—or—desire to do anything to your life."

His gaze lingered on her mouth while an elemental debate warred within him. "Why are you here?"

"To find my brother."

"I can do that *for* you."

"That's not the way I operate."

He rested his palms against the wall and let out the kind of slow breath that indicated strained patience. He leaned down toward her, once more sending aching shafts of desire straight through her. "I'm not used to the way you operate. I don't need you to help me. I've managed quite a few years without a woman tagging along."

Louisiana had been schooled in the corporate boardroom. She had used political savvy and persistent determination to stay where she was. She wasn't about to let this man or any man use sexual maneuvering to gain the upper hand over her.

"I'm not tagging along with anyone—especially with you. I am going to find my brother, and if you care to help, then you can tag along with *me.*" She laid her hands against his chest and pushed him away.

He took the rebuke in calm stride. "You don't know what's involved here, Louisiana."

She brushed some unseen fly away from the front of her blouse and looked over at the downed guard. "So why don't you tell me?"

Gunner's eyes followed her gaze. He hesitated, vacillating between possibilities, then he cursed beneath his breath. "Look, you can go with me to see Roxy. But that's it."

Her response was born of scraped pride. "Oh, sugar, aren't you just the sweetest thing."

He pointed his finger at her, growling from an inner rage he couldn't comprehend. "And don't play those slick magnolia-and-julep games with me. I'm impervious."

In mute anger, he pivoted toward the stairway. Behind him, Louisiana gathered her scattered composure and followed at his heels.

Gunner stepped over the guard, but Louisiana hesitated, all at once unsure of this brash step she had taken. "How long do you think he'll be out?"

"Just long enough, I hope."

She followed him up the stairs and, after reaching the top, he knocked on the door.

There was some light shuffling from inside the room.

He glanced once at Louisiana, then knocked again. "Roxy. It's Gunner. Open up."

"Go 'way," said the timid voice on the other side. "No talk."

"I have to talk to you," said Gunner. "It's about Ham. You know I have to talk to you." He paused, then added, "He's in trouble."

After several long seconds, they finally heard her move across the floor. She slowly slid open the bolt on the door and opened it only a few inches. Gunner rested his foot in the opening to keep it from closing again. The girl stared out at them with wide eyes. She looked at Gunner, but she mostly looked at Louisiana.

"This is Ham's sister, Roxy."

She didn't take her eyes off Louisiana.

"No talk," she said. "Me sick."

"Just for a minute, Roxy. We won't take long. It's important."

After another span of hesitation, she finally opened the door. They stepped into the room and Gunner closed the door behind them. It was a small room, dirty and sparsely furnished. The heat mushroomed up through the floor, making the space feel even smaller. Louisiana examined the surroundings and the girl, searching for a niche in which to fit her. She was a friend of Ham's. But what kind of friend?

Roxy moved away from them, sitting on a lumpy bed in the corner. Gunner moved two chairs over close. Louisiana sat in one. He sat in the other.

"You have to talk to us about Ham, Roxy. You have to tell us what you know."

Her eyes traveled over Louisiana's face and the loose-fitting man's clothes she was wearing. "Hamlin, he tell me he have sister." She glanced at Gunner. "Back in your country."

"This is his sister. Louisiana."

"Hello, Roxy," said Louisiana.

Roxy rolled the name over her tongue, but didn't say it aloud. "Hamlin tell me someday he take me to your country to meet sister. Now I not go to your country."

Gunner leaned forward in his chair and rested his forearms on his knees. "Where is he, Roxy? Does your Uncle Tak have anything to do with this?"

Louisiana looked with a question poised for Gunner, but kept her mouth closed. Tak? Hadn't Bruno said that it had been one of Tak's men who had followed her to Ham's office? She didn't like the fact that Gunner knew more than she did, but her questions would have to wait until later.

Roxy folded her arms across her chest and closed her eyes. "I not work because I am sick. Hamlin, he give me money for medicine. He take me to doctor. Doctor say I can't work for while. Hamlin give me money. I have no money now. Loung Tak, the uncle, he tell me to work good like before so I make money."

Gunner reached into his pocket and pulled out a wad of notes. "Here," he said, pressing them into her hand. "Don't work, Roxy. Just get well. Ham doesn't want you to have to do that kind of work."

Roxy started to cry. She hung her head. "I promise him I not work, but the Uncle Tak, he tell me to work."

"What does Tak have to do with Ham's disappearance? You know something, don't you, Roxy?"

"He first tell me to stay 'way from Hamlin. Then he tell me to stay with Hamlin and tell him everything he say."

"What did you tell your uncle about Ham?"

Roxy looked at Gunner, and Louisiana felt chill bumps slide across her skin when she glimpsed the fear in the girl's face. The girl had told this man—this Uncle Tak—something, and whatever it was it had put her brother in danger.

"Did Ham tell you about the Buddha, Roxy?"

She nodded slowly.

"What did he tell you?"

Her eyes darted from Gunner's face to Louisiana's and back to Gunner's again.

"He tell me it have big secret. Loung Tak want the secret."

"Did he tell you what the secret was?"

"Pictures or words on back of Buddha. They tell of legend."

"What *is* the legend?"

Roxy hesitated. "All Thai people know many legends. But they are just stories."

"But your Uncle Tak believes it is true, doesn't he?"

She nodded.

"And Ham and the abbot believe that it is true?"

She nodded again.

"Tell us the legend, Roxy."

She sat for a long moment and stared at her bony knees protruding from beneath the line of her short black dress. She rested her hands over them. "It was long time ago. Thousand, two thousand year ago, I don't know. Long time. There was a ruler, but no one like him. The Maw Do—the Doctors Who See—say that his son will one day kill him, so the old king have his son thrown out to die. An old woman find the boy and raise him in the jungles. When the boy become man, he overthrow bad ruler and kill him. He marry queen, but when he find out she is mother, he kill her, too. When Buddha die, missionaries come to old kingdom and boy is changed forever. He become defender of faith. He build many temples to Buddha. The kingdom become center of world. And there are many treasures."

When she stopped, Gunner probed for more. "And this Buddha that Ham found tells of these treasures?"

She shrugged. "Fierce warriors from the north come to kingdom and try to take all the Buddhas. They burn the temples. They kill many people. But some monks bury many of the treasures before the bad warriors can find them."

"And Ham believes he knows where they are?"

She shivered. "It is not good to know too much about the gods. It brings evil. Ham should not know so much. It is very bad."

"He told you that he knows where the treasure is buried?"

She shook her head. "It is only story. Many legends in Thailand. Hamlin, he know this. And he cannot understand pictures on Buddha. But his friend, Po, he understand."

"Where is this kingdom supposed to be?"

"In jungles north of Kanchanaburi."

"And Tak wants these treasures, doesn't he?"

She hung her head and a tear fell onto the folds of her dress. "I do not know." Other tears followed. "I know only that he want me to ask Hamlin about Po and about the Buddha."

"Your uncle has a farm."

"My uncle has many rice farms."

"One of them is in the jungles north of Kanchanaburi, isn't it?"

She nodded slowly.

Gunner leaned closer and his voice took on a different tone that Louisiana couldn't decipher. Who was this man Tak? she wondered. And what did a rice farm have to do with hidden treasures? She wished she could follow the train of Gunner's questions.

"Have you ever been there? Roxy, it's very important. I need you to remember. Have you ever been to that farm?"

"Maybe. When I am young girl. I don't know."

"What has Tak told you about Cambodia, Roxy? About refugees?"

Her eyes widened in fright. "I know nothing."

"Has he told you about rubies?"

Louisiana's eyes narrowed on Gunner's face. Rubies? Now what on earth was he talking about? This was absolutely ridiculous. Rubies, rice farms. What did Gunner know that he was not telling her?

Louisiana's body infused with a dry heat as the new thought occurred to her. She stared at Gunner. He had been stringing her along all this time. He knew about Tak and he knew about Ham. He knew what was going on and he hadn't told her. Instead, he had done nothing more than drop tiny morsels for her to scrape up.

Her nerves felt stretched like cold wire as the realization sank in. Gunner knew about Ham and he hadn't bothered to tell her. But why? Why did he not want her to know what had happened to her own brother? Unless...

She stiffened in the chair. Unless he had something to hide. One thing she was certain of, Gunner was involved in all of this. She had thought, through Ham's message, that he wanted her to seek out Gunner for help. But maybe... just maybe he had been trying to

tell her something else entirely. Could she have mis-
interpreted? The thought began to hammer inside her
brain. Was it possible that Gunner was not the one to
help her find Ham, but was instead the one responsible for his disappearance?

She glanced at Roxy. The girl's lip quivered and
tears coursed down her face.

"I know nothing," she cried. "He tell me nothing!"

Gunner sat back and let out a slow, tired breath. He
reached over and laid his hand over hers. "It's okay,
Roxy."

She shook her head and continued to cry softly.
"You must go. If Tak find out I talk to you, he kill
me."

"We'll go."

"My uncle make me tell about statue. I don't want
to tell. When Hamlin find out, he will not love me
anymore. He will be angry with me. I will never see
America."

Louisiana stared at Gunner's fingers as they gently
stroked the girl's hand. Some impulse coiled inside
her, but she could not interpret its message. Things
had meshed together, desire and betrayal. Her body
urged her down one path, while her mind screamed
out its warnings.

She searched Gunner's face for deceit, but found
only tenderness for the girl who, under pressure from
her corrupt uncle, had betrayed Ham. She didn't know
whether to hate her or pity her. Roxy was obviously
someone that Ham cared for, but because of her
weakness she had put him in terrible danger.

Gunner obviously had compassion for the girl. But
was it all a smoke screen to get answers, or was it gen-

uine? Did he have the answers already? She knew when she first met him that he was a man with many secrets. But what were those secrets? And how much danger would Louisiana be in when she learned the truth he seemed determined to hide?

Things are not always what they seem, he had told her. A fair warning. A warning that was obviously meant for her to heed.

When he stood, Louisiana did, also. Roxy looked up with her tearstained face, the black eye makeup trailing in rivulets down her cheeks. She looked at Louisiana this time. "Hamlin want life of good Buddhist. But he love me, too. He not know what he want. But I wait for him to decide." She looked at Gunner. "When you find him, you tell him I wait, okay?"

"Sure, Roxy. I'll tell him."

Louisiana glanced at Gunner's face, so controlled beneath the facade. At the door she turned around once more. Roxy had wrapped her arms around her chest and she rocked slowly back and forth on the bed.

Once outside, Louisiana grasped Gunner's arm and said firmly, "You've got some answers that I want."

Gunner glanced down at the guard. The bulky weight of the man shifted and a low moan came from his throat.

Gunner's gaze shifted to the opposite direction. At the far end of the alley two other men began walking toward them. "Okay," he said, "but first we get the hell out of here."

And all who heard should see them there,
And all should cry, Beware! Beware!
His flashing eyes, his floating hair!

Chapter Seven

Gunner pushed open the door to the Tiger Den and ushered Louisiana inside.

The drinkers stopped and stared, but when they saw her with Gunner, they went back to their own business. A few guys who remembered her from the other night hollered out a rowdy greeting.

Gunner stopped at the bar, ordered a couple of beers and picked up a bowl of cashews.

"What's going on upstairs?" he asked the bartender.

"Movies."

"We need a quiet place."

The bartender glanced at Louisiana and grinned, but when he saw the look on her face, the grin shut down. "There's a room up there that's empty."

"Which one?"

The bartender looked at a list behind the bar. "Number three."

Gunner picked up the beers and handed Louisiana one. "We don't want to be disturbed."

Louisiana was disoriented and unbelievably tired. She didn't know where Gunner was taking her or what he had in mind, but she knew she was going to get some answers. Sparks continued to fly between them, but she refused to let them scramble her judgment. She was no longer sure that he was an ally. For all she knew, he might be the enemy.

They walked through a dark room dominated by a movie screen depicting some sort of bloodbath, accompanied by spitting sounds of gunfire and screams that would curdle milk. Several unfriendly faces stared at the screen, mesmerized.

"What is this?"

"Vietnam," he said. "Some guys just can't let it go."

She followed him up another narrow stairway to a small hall. There were several doors on each side and they stopped at number three. He opened it and, with his hand against her lower back, urged her inside. He flipped on the light and locked the door behind them.

She turned to look at him. "It's a bedroom."

"It's private," he said, moving to the window and pulling the shade to one side. He looked down at the street, then apparently satisfied, let the shade fall back into place. "Have a seat."

Louisiana stood ramrod straight in the center of the room, debating on the best course of action to take with him. She needed answers, and if she alienated him or revealed her mistrust, she might get nothing. Besides, if he was dangerous, this place, this den of cutthroats and mercenaries, was not the place to raise his ire.

Still, her voice retained a cutting edge. "If there was a chair, I would."

"There's a bed," he said, pointing.

She stared at the moth-eaten army blanket that covered the narrow bed. "Thanks, anyway, but I haven't had my shots."

He absorbed the bite of her voice, then went over and sat on the bed, propping his back against the wall. He took a long swig from the bottle of beer. "Suit yourself."

She pursed her lips in thought. "My daddy always said, when you're in a hell of a fix, you go to a saloon, have a drink and fight your way out of it."

Gunner smiled and raised his beer. "I've been in worse fixes."

She looked around the room and then at him. "Why did you bring me here?"

"You don't seem too keen on staying put at your hotel. And this place is somewhat out of harm's way."

Is it? she wondered.

"Besides," he added, "I need time to think."

"And answer questions."

He almost smiled, but the look faded before it actually formed on his face. He held out the bowl of cashews. "Better have some. You haven't had much to eat today."

Her thoughts were more transparent than she would have wished because he added, "This isn't some big seduction scene, if that's what you're wondering." He looked down at the bed he was on. "Not exactly my style."

She looked away and took a drink of beer, hoping to mask the conflagration of feelings. She was filled with fury and fear and fatigue, but they were all overshadowed by other feelings. She thought about the kiss they had shared in the alley and wished fervently that she had not let it happen. If, as he admitted, this was not a seduction scene, then what was it? Had it all been part of a trap that he had so neatly laid and that she had so willingly fallen into? Whatever game he was playing, she was going to find out.

"I have some questions, Gunner. And I'd like straight answers."

"Fire away."

"Tell me about Roxy."

"What do you want to know?"

Louisiana twirled the bottle between her hands. "Does she dance in one of those bars?"

"Yes."

"What else does she do?"

"Do you want to know if she's a prostitute, Louisiana?"

She suddenly wondered if there were things about Ham, about her family, that were better left unknown. She and Ham had both come from the heat of passion. Her own mother had been a stripper in a back-alley jazz club. The nicest thing she could say about Ham's mother was that she was an opportunist. What tainted seeds of character had germinated on those nights so long ago, seeds that had then lain dormant beneath the socially acceptable canopy of Bond prestige and renown?

Reluctantly she nodded.

"Yes, she is. That's what all those girls are."

"I didn't expect Ham to fall for—for a girl like that."

"Relationships take all forms, Louisiana."

"What is that supposed to mean?"

"It means sometimes you have to look beneath surface appearances."

Does that apply to you, too? she wondered, wishing she could confront him with her suspicions, but knowing it was still too soon. *Wise up on all the facts first, darlin',* her daddy always told her. *Then the proper decision can be made.*

"She said she was sick. Does that mean what I think it means?"

"If you mean venereal disease, yes."

"And Ham is paying for her treatments?"

Gunner nodded. "He cares about her, Louisiana. He's even thought about marrying her. It's not unheard of here. American expats marry Thai girls all the time."

She closed her eyes briefly, awash with fatigue. There were so many things still to ask him. There were questions about rubies and Cambodia and rice farms. "Tell me about this man Tak."

"He's the minister of public works. Here that means he's in charge of restoration of the *wats.*"

"The temples?"

"Loosely speaking, a *wat* is a Buddhist monastery. It's usually a large walled compound that includes a bot where the Buddha image is kept, the spired cone-shaped domes called *chedis*, monks' lodging and sometimes a government school."

"Okay, so Tak makes sure these are in tip-top shape, right?"

"Well, he doesn't do much with the temples himself. It's a political position."

"What does his position have to do with Ham?"

Gunner paused, then shrugged. "It has to do with greed."

Louisiana took another drink of beer, working the thought around in her mind. "Something you're acquainted with?"

He stared at her for a long moment. The air between them hung thick and bold with the scent of a lingering passion. She felt it pervading her skin, writhing its way through her thoughts until the physical urges she felt for him became entwined with the suspicions and doubts.

"Come sit down, Louisiana. You look exhausted."

She walked with leaden feet to the bed and sat down. "I have so many more questions, Gunner," she said softly. "So many things I need to know."

He handed her his beer. "Here, hold this."

She took it and he brushed her long blond hair aside, then laid his hands on her shoulders. His fingers, like heated tines, dug deeply into her muscles and, despite her wish to stay alert and focused, she let her head drop forward and her eyes close. She gave in to the heat from his hands. "You've done this before, I can tell. Is this what they call a Thai massage?"

Those deft fingers moved up her neck and over the back of her head. "This is the traditional kind. There is another . . . if you're interested."

Invisible fingers slid to more intimate places in her mind. "I thought you said this room wasn't your style."

His hands slid over her shoulders and down her arms, kneading the muscles. His voice was distant and gravelly. "Well, as you said last night, there's always a first time for everything. Besides, we locals like to accommodate the eager tourists."

She smiled. "I'll just bet you do."

The fingers stopped moving. They lay motionless against her arms. She felt his breath on the back of her neck. Her own breath was caught and held in her throat.

This is crazy! she told herself. *I don't even trust this guy! I am here to find my brother, that's all. Nothing more. But those fingers!*

She turned around slowly and faced him. "I don't know where to go next, Gunner. I don't know what steps to take."

His hands slid like hot oil down her arms to the bed. His eyes focused on her mouth while a battle of options raged within him. The years of training won out and he finally chose the one that would lead to success and survival.

"Haven't you had enough, Louisiana?"

"I'm not going home, Gunner. A Bond does not tuck her tail between her legs and run away."

"You don't know what you're up against."

"So tell me, then. Is it Tak? Is he the one I have to watch out for?" *Or is it you?* she silently added.

"It was one of Tak's men who tried to kill you today."

"But why?"

"Because he either doesn't want you sniffing around after your brother or he doesn't want you talking to me."

"But you haven't told me what Ham and Tak have to do with each other. I mean, I know that Ham found this statue that turns out to be jade instead of plaster. And because it's got some inscription or whatever on the back that he can't read, he takes it to his teacher—what's his name?"

"Po."

"Right, Po. And Ham makes the mistake of telling Roxy about this Buddha. Then Roxy tells her uncle. But how did Tak know there was a Buddha statue? I mean, what made him tell Roxy to find out about it in the first place?"

He stood and walked to the window, pulling aside the shade to once again peer down at the street below. There was a sharp knock at the door. Louisiana's gaze flew to Gunner's face. The shade dropped back into place. He stood tensed, poised for action.

"It's okay," he whispered. "They wouldn't have let just anybody know where we were." He held up his hand. "Don't move." He advanced on silent feet to the door. Standing to the side of the door, his back against the wall, his voice shot cold and hard into the air. "Yeah."

Some unintelligible mumble came from the other side, but Gunner sighed in relief and flung open the door. Bruno lumbered into the room, holding Roxy in the crook of his arm.

"Oh, my God!" cried Louisiana, jumping off the bed. Roxy's eye sported an ugly bruise and her cheek was swollen to twice its normal size. Her knee looked scraped and raw and the torn sleeve of her dress hung over her shoulder.

The girl's knees collapsed beneath her just as Gunner reached for her. He carried her to the bed and set her on it. "Grab that towel over there, Louisiana. And get it wet."

Louisiana grabbed the towel that was hung over a wooden bar by the sink. She wet it thoroughly and brought it back to the bed. Gunner took it and laid it against Roxy's cheekbone.

He looked at Bruno. "What happened?"

"Tak's men," said Bruno. "I followed them to her room."

Gunner pushed her hair back from her face. "They must have come right after we left. What did you tell them, Roxy?"

She began to cry again. "They kill me if I talk to you. They say they will kill me."

Louisiana stepped forward and knelt down in front of her. "Roxy, Ham is in trouble. You have to tell us."

At the sound of her voice, Roxy stopped crying. She raised her eyes and stared into Louisiana's face.

"I know you care about him," Louisiana continued. "I care about him, too. He's my brother and I love him very much. You have to help me find him."

Roxy sniffled. She glanced at Gunner and at Bruno, then her eyes shifted back to Louisiana. "They hurt me and I'm lying on the floor. They don't know I am listening. But they say the Uncle Tak has gone to his rice farm. They say he has gone to take care of the little abbot."

Louisiana grabbed Gunner's arm. "If the abbot is there, then Ham has to be there, too."

Gunner kept his attention on Roxy. "Did they ask you if we'd been to see you?"

"Yes."

"What did you tell them, Roxy?"

Her frightened eyes flitted from one person in the room to the other. "They think you know something about Kampuchea." She glanced at Louisiana. "Cambodia." She looked back at Gunner. "I—they do not tell me what you know. And I not know. Ham, he tell me something, but it doesn't make sense to me. So I tell them this. I tell them I know nothing, but they don't believe me. They hit me, so I tell them that you are looking for Ham and abbot. They tell me they going to kill you. Tak say they must kill you."

She looked at Louisiana. "They say they are going to kill you, too. Tak very angry that you are not dead." She turned to Gunner. "Uncle Tak is bad man. He hurt people very bad. He hurt Ham's sister if he catch her."

Louisiana felt panic bubbling through her bloodstream, but Gunner's quiet voice had the necessary calming effect. "No one is going to hurt her, Roxy. I'll make sure of that." The only hint of anger was in the crushing grip of his hand around the towel. He threw it across the room and stood, turning to Bruno.

"We'll go tonight."

Bruno nodded. "The boat waits at the dock."

"Yes, your boat's better. Tak's men will no doubt be watching the train station."

Bruno's head bobbed toward the women. "What about them?"

Gunner thought for a moment. "Louisiana can't go back to her hotel. They'll be waiting there. I'll take both of them to Victoria's. They'll be safe there."

"Excuse me," Louisiana interjected, the anger and suspicion moving to the forefront once again. "You're not taking me anywhere except to find my brother."

Gunner let out a slow breath, aimed at drawing patience. "I know now where he is, Louisiana. And the Kanchanaburi province is no place for you. But I'll find him, I promise."

"Without me."

"Yes," he growled harshly. "Without you."

Her smirk was one of disbelief. "You still don't get it, do you, Gunner? I'm not a watcher. I'm not one to sit back on the sidelines and watch problems resolve themselves. My daddy didn't raise me that way. And Ham is *my* brother.''

Gunner stepped closer. "There is more at stake here than just your brother.''

"Oh, yeah, what? Maybe some rubies you want to get your hands on?''

Gunner's eyes narrowed dangerously, but he worked hard to keep his temper in check. "I'm taking you to a friend's apartment. She's with the British council. You'll like her. And you and Roxy will be safe with her. She can arrange to get your clothes from the hotel and get you on a plane.''

Her face was only inches from his, and despite his quiet tone, she felt the heat of anger emanating from his skin. Her chin lifted marginally. "And if I don't go?''

His eyes blazed hotly and fired her skin like twin forges. "Then,'' he said with that deadly calm of his, "you might just find yourself at the mercy of Tak or his men. Not a merciful group.''

She stared into his face, but she felt clammy fingers of fear steal across her flesh. If he was trying to scare her off the trail, he was doing a damn good job of it. But something had been added to this game of hide-and-seek, something personal and intimate. And one thing she had learned from her daddy was that, as a Bond, she must never forfeit a game—never quit...not until she had won.

AT ONE TIME, it had been a warehouse. And Louisiana thought it still looked like one, although it had been spruced up with a chandelier in the entry and the stairway had been buffed to a suntanned glow. The halls were wide, with only three or four spacious apartments opening onto each floor.

At the far end of the hallway, Gunner stopped and knocked on a door. When the door swung open, music spilled out from the apartment. Cigarette smoke hung in a thick cloud cover over the room. Dozens of people, in the midst of chugging drinks and fondling one another with the camaraderie of happy drunks, were oblivious to the intruders.

"Oh, luv—hullo!" The doorway framed a tall attractive woman with short dark hair that circled a round face and bright blue eyes. Victoria grabbed the front of Gunner's shirt, pulling him close, and pressed her lips against his.

"A party, I see," Gunner murmured indulgently when she released his lips.

"Well, the council is closed tomorrow. Lord Peter's birthday and all. Since the embassy's taking a holiday, we thought—why not us, too?"

Gunner smiled. "Why not, indeed."

"Of course, luv, if I'd known you were going to show up, I would have planned a more intimate party—without all these people."

Gunner pulled Victoria into the hallway where she was confronted with three bedraggled houseguests. "Listen, Vic," he said more seriously, "I need your help."

The party face fell away, leaving one that was all business. "Right," she said matter-of-factly. "What can I do?"

"This is Louisiana Bond. Ham's sister. And this is Roxy. They need a place to stay. A safe place."

Victoria gave Louisiana the once-over and cast a sly glance at Gunner. "They always have to be pretty, don't they?"

He grinned and lightly grasped Louisiana's arm, saying to her, "This is Victoria Burton. You'll be safe here."

They exchanged perfunctory greetings, but Louisiana didn't feel right about this whole setup. Disregarding the unfamiliar and unwelcome stab of jealousy, she wondered what Victoria's part was in all of this. She hadn't asked Gunner why the two women needed a safe place; she hadn't even shown surprise. Aside from the obvious personal relationship between Victoria and Gunner, there was also a professional one. But what? She was British; Gunner said she worked for some British council. She knew Ham. She obviously knew of Roxy. What role could she play in finding Ham? Or, perhaps more appropriately, what role had she played in his disappearance?

Victoria gave them another quick appraisal, her lips thinning at the sight of Roxy's bruised and battered face. "Of course they can stay. You don't mind the couch, do you?" she asked Louisiana.

"Not at all," Louisiana said. It wasn't the couch she minded. It was the fact of being here at all. She had no intention of sitting around for several days with one of Gunner's *gals* when her brother was in danger. No way. She was going to find out what Gunner was up to. And she was going to make sure that Ham's welfare was everyone's primary concern.

"You'll both need clothes," Victoria said. She turned to Gunner. "Any special instructions?"

"Send someone to the Oriental to get her things and . . . well, just watch your backside."

Victoria smiled. "I always do, luv."

She turned to her unexpected guests. "Well, then, as you can see—and hear—it's going to be a late night here tonight. But in there is the loo. And help yourself to whatever you can find in the fridge."

Louisiana stepped into the apartment, but she stopped and watched as Victoria looped her arm through Gunner's and spoke softly. "You can stay the night, too, you know, luv."

Gunner turned toward her and smiled. "Can't."

She sighed. "No. Of course not. You never can, can you?"

Gunner smiled. "Come on, Vic, you know I'm just saving myself from heartbreak down the road."

Louisiana watched Victoria's mouth form an indignant pout. "Is that the kind of reputation I have? Have all you Yanks been talking behind my back?"

Gunner rested his hand on the doorsill, grinning as he leaned close. "There are a few gentlemen left in this world, you know."

Victoria sighed loudly. "Lord, I hope you're not going to be one of them." She shook her head. "You and Bruno, what a pair. I suppose you're going off in that dink of his?"

Gunner's eyes shifted quickly to where Louisiana was standing a few feet away, then back to Victoria. "As you know, we've got some business to take care of."

"Business." Victoria sighed. "Always business. Well, bring me a trinket."

She slipped back into the apartment and disappeared in the crowd of rowdy guests. Roxy followed Victoria, looking lost and miserable. Louisiana didn't budge. She stared at Gunner, hating herself for these irrational stirrings of jealousy and for her own feelings of loneliness, and disliking him for putting her in this position. Victoria was in on information that Louisiana had no access to. Whatever Gunner knew, he wasn't telling her. That could only mean one thing: whatever he knew or was up to, he wasn't telling Louisiana because she would not approve. The significance of that fact did not bode well for Ham.

Misinterpreting her stare, Gunner said, "You'll be okay here. You don't have to be afraid."

"Fear has nothing to do with it. I am simply not staying."

Gunner took her arm and pulled her back out into the hall, away from the light from the apartment. With her back against the flocked paper, he flattened both palms against the wall on each side of her. "Listen to me, Louisiana. And listen good. You have to stay out of this."

"Oh, do I really? And what about my brother?"

Gunner hesitated only slightly. "I'll find him."

He was so close, his face only inches from hers, and she sensed the rapid rise and fall of his breath. His eyes spoke of the hot jungle, of the waiting dark, of something primitive and hungry that stalked in the night. She forced a calmness into her voice that she did not feel. "Not much slips by me, Gunner."

His eyes centered on her mouth, where they remained for several seconds before returning to her eyes. "I've noticed. But on this one you're just going to have to trust me."

"Well, like I already told you, my daddy taught me to trust no one."

With a final uncertain stare, Gunner turned and walked away, heading down the hallway toward the stairs. But before he reached them, he heard her final parting shot. "And I always do what my daddy taught me."

She watched him disappear down the stairs, leaving her behind . . . to trust him. Well, she had a news flash for him—she didn't trust him any farther than she could throw him. She wasn't used to depending on men. She didn't want to have to start now. And just because being around him made her feel as if she were sinking in quicksand, she wasn't going to let it affect her decisions. She had come to find her brother. And that was exactly what she was going to do.

Closing the apartment door, Louisiana went in search of Roxy and Victoria. She found them in the bedroom where Victoria was laying out a skirt and blouse for Roxy to wear.

"I have something here for you, too," she said when Louisiana came into the room.

"I won't be needing them. Listen, Victoria. I want you to tell me where they've gone."

Victoria turned around slowly, a half smile on her lips. "Where that man goes, nobody knows."

"This is important."

"I'm aware of that."

Louisiana walked over to where Roxy sat ill at ease on the corner of the bed. She bent down. "Roxy, you've got to tell me. They said something about a boat. Bruno's boat. Do you know where he docks it?"

"No, Roxy," warned Victoria. "Don't say anything. Gunner wants you both to stay here."

"Roxy," urged Louisiana. "It's for Ham. You want us to find him, don't you? Please help me."

Roxy's eyes darted from one equally determined woman to the other. She wasn't used to choices. They had always been made for her.

"It's at Dock Maharat," she said softly. "By Phra Pinklao Bridge."

"Does the boat have a name or identifying mark of any kind?"

Roxy glanced once again at Victoria's grim face. "Green. Green boat."

Louisiana touched her lightly. "Thank you, Roxy."

"I could use force to keep you here," said Victoria.

"What, some brute out there in your living room?" Louisiana shook her head. "You won't."

"Gunner doesn't like being countermanded."

"Tough."

Victoria sighed. "You don't know what you're getting into."

"Maybe not. But at least I'll be doing something. I appreciate your hospitality, but I can't stay here."

Victoria gave Louisiana a long look of quiet appraisal. "Tell Gunner I tried, will you?"

Louisiana nodded. "I will." She moved to the door.

Victoria called out, "If you do find the boat, they won't let you come aboard, you know."

Louisiana didn't hear. She was already out the door.

Five miles meandering with a mazy motion
Through wood and dale the sacred river ran

Chapter Eight

The taxi jerked to a stop at the end of Na Prathat Road. The sky was dark, the night veiled in a murky mist. Louisiana paid the driver and got out amid his protests. At least, she assumed they were protests. He spoke little English, but his gestures and tone indicated that this was no place for a woman to be alone. Still, she had to find Bruno's boat. She wasn't going to sit around in Victoria Burton's apartment, relying on Gunner and on chance.

"Maharat?" she asked the driver through the window.

He frowned, not understanding.

"Phra Pinklao," she tried, pointing to the bridge that spanned two segments of the mist-shrouded Chao Phya River.

He shrugged. "No speak English."

"I'm not speaking English," she mumbled. She thought she was saying it the same way Roxy had. But the tonal languages of the East were not the easiest ones for Westerners to master.

"*Khapkhun*," she said, thanking him and, looping her purse over her shoulder, picked her way through the dark.

She felt the squish of soft ground beneath her feet and heard the light tap of boats that bumped against one another where they were moored at the water's edge.

As her eyes adjusted to the darkness, and as she drew nearer to boats with lanterns and small fires burning, she saw children curled up asleep on teak barges, while men murmured to one another as they pulled in fishing lines to see if anything edible had attached itself to them. Women leaned over the boats, rinsing enamel plates and bowls in the muddy water.

The ground grew softer nearer the water and she worried about what she might step on. In the two days since she had been in Bangkok, she had seen everything from dead animals to tires floating down the river and canals. And if snakes were milling about on the downtown sidewalks, it was a sure bet there were one or two slithering around down here.

Dismay hit her full force when she realized how all the boats looked the same. A green boat, Roxy had said. Big deal. There were probably thirty or forty green boats tied up to the dock, although on each the hue had long ago worn away to thin fading strips of lime here and there. The boats were all pretty much the same. Flat and low to the water with broad canvas covers arching over the tops—family homes, decorated with photographs and battery-operated wall clocks and with laundry hung from poles attached to the sides.

She moved slowly down the dock, aware of hundreds of eyes following her every step. She was never going to find Bruno's boat here. And glancing back toward the road, she realized she would never find a taxi to take her back to Victoria's. This was not exactly the theater district. There was no line of yellow cabs waiting like a string of buttered popcorn against the curb.

She took a deep breath and quelled the nausea that was beginning to rise in her stomach. The question to ask herself, she knew, was what would Daddy Bond have done? *Daughter, when you're in a wild bull's pasture without a tree, you run like hell.* She glanced back, but saw no place to run to.

She kept walking, trying not to stare at the half-naked forms strewn upon their barges like pieces of seaweed the tide had washed in. But each step she took sounded loud and heavy to her ears. Farther ahead, shielded behind the thick dark mist, were men's voices. They were muffled and she could only make out indistinct figures moving like exaggerated shadows from the dock to the bow of a boat, loading boxes.

She stopped and listened until she confirmed the voice in her mind. Gunner was speaking, but she couldn't catch the words. She hung back, hidden from them by the dark and by their own preoccupation with their task.

Once finished loading boxes, they climbed into the rocking boat and shifted everything from the front to the back.

Louisiana inched forward, straining to hear their voices. They were not in the front of the boat. They were either in the cabin or at the stern.

A lantern hung from the canvas top and she could see all the way through to the rear. They were standing together, hauling something from one box and sliding another box into a niche against the side of the boat.

She stepped onto the barge, crouching down and grabbing the edge of the bow for support against the rocking motion. As she eased down in the boat, she realized that there was at least an inch of water where she squatted. She crept forward, keeping her eyes on the two men as she wriggled her way toward the center of the boat. There was a blanket in front of her, so she crawled to it and drew it over her body.

It smelled like something that had been dead for a week and she thought she might choke from the stink. Swallowing a cough, she lay very still, hoping they wouldn't need the blanket before they shoved off from the dock.

Seconds passed like hours while Gunner and Bruno walked the length of the boat, organizing and strapping everything down to their satisfaction.

The mist turned to rain. The water dripped through the blanket's thin veneer, soaking her clothes and skin.

"Okay," she heard Gunner say. "Let's get out of here."

No sooner had the words left his mouth when a thundering shout pierced the night. From under the hot, sweaty blanket, Louisiana heard footsteps hammering down the dock and angry voices calling out, "*Yout! Yout!* Stop!"

Gunner cursed and yelled something to Bruno. His heavy feet pounded within inches of Louisiana's head as he rushed to the bow to untie the rope lashed to the pier. Inside the cabin, Gunner cursed and tore into one of the boxes. He dashed outside and she heard a metallic click and slide.

There was another shout, then a loud pop.

Gunner and Bruno were scrambling around and men on the dock were shouting. It took several seconds for Louisiana to realize that the punctuated bursts she was hearing were gunfire. A bullet landed less than an inch from her head and she screamed. She threw the blanket from her body and scrambled to her knees, trying to claw her way through the driving rain toward the cabin.

A string of curses spewed from Gunner's mouth. The guns continued to flare and spit into the wet night and Louisiana's terror was trapped in her throat. She couldn't make her knees move fast enough as she tried to scramble into the cabin.

She felt something hard and heavy land on top of her and the air rushed out of her lungs. She was pressed down into the boat, her face buried in a coil of rope, the pressure on her body so heavy she couldn't breathe. Her ears rang and she thought she was going to faint.

She could feel the boat sliding out into the canal as a new string of bullets were fired into the hull. She instinctively tried to curl up in a ball, but the weight on top of her kept her straight and flat. She felt heavy breathing against her scalp and neck and she knew that it was a person lying on her. She felt him shift and the blast from a gun went off just above her left ear. Her scream was nothing more than a muffled squeak and she tasted the musty threads of hemp in her mouth.

When she thought she would surely pass out, the weight lifted. The ringing in her ears subsided and the sounds of gunfire faded away into the mists.

She tried to kneel, panic and fear still transmitting the message to escape. A sound came from her throat, something between a cry and a moan.

Hands clutched her waist and held on to her, turning her onto her back. Through her tears, she saw Gunner pull her to him with a desperate look on his face.

"My God! Louisiana!" His voice was like a turbulent wind. The rain ran in rivulets down his face and neck, forming a pool where it fell in the hollow of her neck. "Are you okay? Are you hurt?"

His arm was around her waist, holding her beneath him while his other hand stroked her hair. She wanted to tell him that she was fine, but the fear kept her from speaking. She clutched the front of his shirt, gripping it between her wet fingers and trying to form words in her clogged throat.

His hand continued to stroke her wet hair as he hauled her closer, his wet body molding to hers. He breathed heavily against her neck, his mouth hot and moist against her throat. The boat rocked into the night as they held on to each other.

It was much too soon when he let her loose. He reached up for the lantern and pulled it down, holding it over her. His eyes scanned the length of her, checking for wounds. "You didn't get hit, did you?"

She shook her head. "I—I don't think so." She looked up as Bruno came and stood over them, a heavy gun still gripped in his hand. "What she is doing here?" he growled.

Gunner let out a ragged breath and his look of concern evolved into a dark scowl. "Yes, what the hell *are* you doing here!"

She sat up and backed against the side of the boat, wiping the rain from her face with a shaking hand. "I told you I wasn't staying behind," she snapped, her voice too high and tight. She felt vulnerable and defensive and at the mercy of some fate that had slipped completely from her grasp.

"What we do with her?" grumbled Bruno.

Gunner stood and stared at her as if she were something slimy and unclean dangling from a fisherman's net. "Hell if I know," he grumbled and stalked into the cabin, leaving her to fend off Bruno's malevolent glare.

She managed to lift herself to her feet, but her legs were still wobbly. Grabbing hold of the metal rods that held the canvas cover in place, she staggered past Bruno without looking at him and ducked in under the canvas cover. The rain beat against the roof and perforated its skin with tiny pinpoints of water leaking throughout the cabin.

Louisiana couldn't remember when she had ever felt so miserable in all her life. She glanced back at Bruno, still staring at her as if he was debating whether to throw her overboard with the night's garbage or shoot her with the gun that still dangled from his fingers.

She looked at Gunner. He was standing at the stern, swiveling the arm of the motor so that the barge moved to the center of the river where it sliced a clean line against the current. He wore a hat and the rain dripped from its brim like a showerhead.

She carefully made her way to the back and stood next to Gunner in the rain. He glanced down at her, then made another adjustment to the motor. His mouth was tight, his profile grim, as he stared at the water kicked up by their wake.

"How did you find us?" he asked in a quiet voice.

"Roxy told me where the boat was docked." She shrugged. "I took a cab."

He glanced at her with disbelieving eyes. "You came by yourself to the dock at night?"

"I wanted to find you."

"You could have been shot. They meant to kill us, you know."

"Who were they?"

"Tak's men." Gunner glanced back at Bruno, who was kneeling back inside the cabin, drying off the gun and putting it away. He called out to him, "How many did we get?"

"Only one, I think" came the answer.

Gunner sighed. "We haven't seen the end of them, you can count on that."

"You mean they'll try to follow us?" she asked, aware of a warble in her throat.

"I mean they'll do whatever it takes to finish the job."

She swallowed loudly. "Thank you," she said to Gunner, her voice weaker than she wished it would sound.

"For what?" he grumbled.

"For covering me—with your body."

His mumbled reply was gruff and unintelligible.

"And for holding me afterward," she added softly.

He stared out over the water. "No problem."

She remembered distinctly the feel of his body pressed against hers, and she knew that there had been something driving him besides a sense of duty. "No problem" didn't quite cover the physical reaction she had felt in him.

"Why did you let go, Gunner? Why did you walk away?"

He sighed impatiently. "Look, near-death experiences make some people religious. They have a different effect on me, okay?"

Her mouth tightened. "I see." She turned and picked her way slowly and carefully into the covered cabin. Bruno was patching a hole in the side of the barge with something that Louisiana hoped was official nautical glue but that looked more like chewing gum.

She found a narrow bench and sat down, wondering miserably how she was going to endure the two men's morose silence and bitterness toward her. She stared at a rice cake on a tiny counter and couldn't remember the last time she had eaten. Her stomach growled, but Bruno, thank God, didn't hear. What she would give now for a big old barbecued beef sandwich and stuffed baked potato, a side of cole slaw, some dewberry pie and a huge glass of iced tea! Real food in Texas-size portions, that's what she craved.

She also wished she had some dry clothes, a hairbrush, a nice soft bed to lie in. She would have had those, she realized now, if she had stayed at Victoria's. She could have been dry and safe and full. But, no, she had to dash off into flying bullets and driving rain instead. Great idea, Louisiana!

At the back of the boat, Gunner concentrated on keeping the barge in the middle of the river. If he kept his mind on the task at hand, he wouldn't have to think about what was really bothering him.

Why was she here? He wasn't used to people disobeying his orders, especially women. He realized he hadn't really given orders to many women in his life, but he'd always assumed that if he had, they would obey the same way men under his command always

had, with blind obedience. Why wouldn't Louisiana
Bond do the same? She could easily have been shot.
Ham's sister, killed while in his camp. It was unthink-
able.

He glanced into the cabin where the lantern swayed
with the motion of the boat. She sat beneath it, on a
bench, silently watching Bruno work on the bullet
holes in the wood. She looked lost and afraid and, for
the first time since he'd met her, completely vulnerable.

It wasn't that she usually acted macho. It was just
that she wielded so much power and still did it in such
a feminine way. He wasn't used to it. In the East, men
had the power and women offered solace and softness. Louisiana Bond was a complicated mix of both.

And stubborn! She had no idea what she was involved in. She had no idea where this would lead any
of them. Or did she? Maybe she was playing some
game of her own. What the hell had Ham said about
him, anyway?

She had guts; he had to give her that. Just like Ham.
Always jumping into the frying pan without first
checking to see how hot the fire was. He and Louisiana might be only half brother and sister, but they
were definitely offshoots of the same root stock. Billy
Boone Bond must have been one tough old bean.

"Bruno."

Louisiana and Bruno looked up at the same time
when Gunner called him.

"Take over, would you."

Bruno stood and walked out to the stern. He took
the steering arm from Gunner.

Louisiana watched the transfer of command with
tired eyes. She could barely keep hers open. It had

been the longest day she could ever remember. Now all she wanted was to curl up on one of the pallets that lay along the port side and go to sleep.

Gunner ducked beneath the canvas. He glanced at Louisiana, then bent and pulled a bottle from a box on the floor. He held it up. "*Mekhong.* Our version of Yukon Jack. Care for a drink?"

Her half smile was slow in coming, but it did come. "Where did you get that?"

"Brought it along, just in case we needed it for medicinal purposes."

"Right."

He rummaged around until he found a couple of cups. When he did, he set them on the counter and poured liquid into each. "The rain has stopped."

She looked to the front of the boat. She hadn't even noticed. She had gone from drenched to miserable to lethargic and there she had stayed.

He reached for her hand and pulled her to her feet. He handed her both cups and he took down the lantern from its hook. Carrying it, he led the way to the front of the boat. She followed, walking carefully down the rocking water-logged barge.

"Here's a dry spot," said Gunner, pulling out a blanket to sit on.

"I didn't think there was a dry spot in all of Thailand," she retorted.

"Well, let's just say it's less wet."

He set the lantern down, took the cups from her and waited until she was settled before he sat down beside her. He handed her a cup and watched her take a small dainty sip, not at all like the way she had gulped it down at the Tiger Den.

The sky was thick and hot. It felt like a weight on her shoulders.

"Are you okay?" he asked.

"Just tired." She sighed loudly. "It has been one hell of a day."

"It has been that." He grinned. "So Louisiana Bond—you feel like you're in Asia now?"

She took another sip of the whiskey and her throat constricted from the burn. "I feel like I'm in the middle of a Francis Ford Coppola movie." She closed her eyes briefly and took a deep breath. "Tell me about Victoria."

He frowned and poured some more whiskey into their cups. "What do you want to know?"

"She didn't seem all that shocked when you showed up with Roxy and me. You must have dumped distressed women on her before."

"We help each other out from time to time."

"What does she do for the British council?"

He shrugged. "Cultural liaison."

Louisiana stared down into her cup, then lifted her eyes to Gunner. "She's some sort of undercover agent, isn't she?"

He took a hefty swig. "You've read too many spy novels."

"I think that's why I'm so tired," she said.

He frowned. "From reading too much?"

"No." She looked directly into his eyes. "From never getting a straight answer from you."

When he made no response, she looked away. "I didn't know there would be guns. You must have been expecting them to come after you here."

"We knew they might."

"You could have been killed, too."

"That was a possibility. I like to think of it as a remote one."

She glanced up to see that he was smiling at her. She said, "You're very sure of yourself, aren't you?"

"If you don't know who you are and what you want, you have no business being in this part of the world."

"And what do you want?"

This was getting into an area he was less secure about. Just being near her made him think about other places and other ways of life. She made him think of softness and pleasures and endless nights under a blanket of stars. She made him want something he had no business wanting.

He took a big drink of whiskey, but it didn't help. He looked at her and his hand lifted. He fingered a wet strand of her hair. "When I was a kid, I wanted to do the right thing. I wanted to see the world." He shrugged.

Something tightened inside of her when he twisted a strand of her hair around his finger. She tried to keep her breath even and steady, but an electric charge shot through her and she inhaled deeply. "And now?" she managed, holding her breath.

There was a pause. "The focus has changed somewhat." He reached for the bottle and poured another shot into their cups.

"I don't really like this stuff," she said, but she took a sip, anyway.

"No?"

She shook her head. "No. I grew up with men, though. My friends drank wine spritzers. I drank beer and whiskey. It was what my daddy expected."

"Maybe it was what you thought he expected."

The notion took her by surprise, but as it settled in, she saw that maybe Gunner was right. "I wanted to fit into his world."

"You know," he said carefully, "sometimes you have to look at what *you* like instead of what other people like."

She lowered her eyes and stared at the coil of rope on the other side, the same pile of rope she had lain on when bullets were zinging around her head.

His hands lifted her hair away from her neck and the wind rushing by them breathed across her skin.

"What do you like, Louisiana?"

She closed her eyes, hoping he would never move his hand from the back of her head. "I think—I think I like to feel safe."

A long space of silence stretched between them. His fingers lay against her scalp, unmoving. Slowly he set down his cup and took hers from her hand. He set it down a foot away.

Her breath dangled like the fronds of a palm tree over water, suspended, hanging, seeking moisture.

His free hand rested on her thigh, his fingers molding to the wet cotton fabric. His hand slid upward, sliding ever so slowly along the side of her hip, across her waist and onto her rib cage. Her heart found a new beat. Her blood pulsated just below the surface of her skin. She was aware of every current of hot air that sailed over her. The grind of the motor grew deeper and more steady.

"Do you feel safe now?" he asked quietly, his voice a hypnotic blend of the night and the heat and the jungle that loomed on both sides of them. "With me?"

She forced her eyes upward to his. He was so close, his mouth so near to hers, the brown of his eyes so dark and primitive in the yellow glow of the lantern. Her breath fell against his chin. "No," she whispered. "Not at all."

His mouth fastened over hers, his lips warm, rich, tasting faintly of whiskey and salt. She laid her hand against his neck. It was hot and moist. Her fingers ran down the front of his shirt, crumpling it in her hand as it dropped. He lowered her body and, at the same time, reached for the lantern, extinguishing the light. The dark was impenetrable, like wet wool, and it urged them deeper into the belly of the barge. His hand slid between them, his fingers kneading her breasts like clay until his mouth took over. His touch was exploratory and unhurried, moving with the flow and rhythm of the river down which they skimmed. Their breaths mingled, their infrequent murmurings merged. He held her cradled against the hard wood. She wrapped herself around him.

There were no more thoughts of mistrust or of lies. There were only two people, two survivors who needed each other. She had never needed a man in the same way she now needed him, and he gave her all that she longed for and more.

She sank into his arms and into the night and knew that she would never feel this safe again.

The shadow of the dome of pleasure
Floated midway on the waves;
Where was heard the mingled measure
From the fountain and the caves.

Chapter Nine

It was the Hindu deity Garuda, with its head and legs of a bird and its body and arms of a man, holding a powerless snake in its grasp, that finally made it clear where he was. Ham had not noticed the sculpture before. It had been too dark and his swollen eyes had refused to open.

From where he lay, he heard the sound of water dripping slowly, but it seemed very far off. There was another sound, too, a low hum of sorts, but he could not place it. In intermittent moments of consciousness, he regained patches of memory, but he could not put them into a logical sequence.

There had been an early-morning mist hanging in folds over the hills. Po had been holding a shovel. They had made a long climb, difficult and tiring. The soldiers around them had laughed.

Ham's eyes were closed, but they could not shut out the memories. There was so little Po could tell the soldiers. He was the keeper of the legend, the bearer of the tale, that was all. But they had pushed the shovel into Po's hand. They had called the abbot a liar. "He will dig," one of them had said. "He will dig until he dies."

The memories faded and, for long periods of time, Ham heard and saw nothing. Later, as if he were swimming up from the depths of some murky *klong,* his bruised eyes began to adjust to the hell in which he had been cast. A slim shaft of light shifted through an opening in the rocks above him. A small depression in the stone beside him held a shallow pool of water, fed by a continuous drip from the rock ceiling above. It took several minutes to maneuver his body, but finally he was able to angle over onto his stomach and suck up a little of the stagnant liquid. He rolled back over, exhausted from the effort.

Sometime later he stretched out his arm, sliding his hand along the moist, cool floor. He reached a wall, but his strength left him and his hand fell to the floor, landing on something long and smooth. With great effort, he dragged it close, holding it in front of his eyes. His fingers tensed and the object fell from his grasp.

Lying on the damp floor that smelled of decaying earth and molded stone, Ham stared at the long smooth bone in front of him. His horrified gaze lifted to the wall. The massive gold sculpture of the Garuda was flanked by skeletons, human ones, dozens of them, hanging by iron chains in the carved-out niches in the wall.

The Buddha taught that life was suffering and disappointment from which a wise man must seek to deliver himself. Was this the way, then, that he would find release from the endless cycle of birth and death? In this cave of rotting martyrs?

To do so, he must find complete absence of all physical consciousness, all thought, all will. But he could not. He was still conscious of the throbbing in his pain-racked body, and his thoughts were anything but serene. He didn't want to die. He didn't want his life to end as nothing more than bleached, calcified bones. There was still so much to see and do. There were too many sins for which he needed to find recompense.

He had failed his father. He had never been able to live up to the expectations of the inimitable Billy Boone Bond.

In his father's mind, he had gone off to fight in unpopular wars. He claimed that Ham had sided, at times, with the antithesis of capitalism and colonialism. He had fought against many of the things his own father revered. They had never shared the truth between them. But he had always loved his father. He wished now that he had found a way to show it.

He thought about Louisiana and, for the first time, envied the security of her life back in Texas. He had forgotten about the message he had sent her. His mind was filled with nothing but pleasant memories of her. He saw her sitting on the tailgate of a pickup, boots dangling off the end. He heard her easy laughter. He smiled to himself at the picture of her, happy and safe on their big ranch back home.

He became aware of the low humming sound again. He shifted his head and could just make out the small figure sitting across the cave. The man's back was against the wall, his head was tilted forward, his eyes closed. A low, soft chant came from deep inside his chest.

"Po," whispered Ham, but the sound did not leave his throat. His eyes fastened on the abbot, and he listened to the reassuring sound of meditation. He watched him in silence, not wanting to disturb the man's peace. If only he, too, could find that kind of peace for himself.

Dazed and racked with pain, Ham lay back against the ground and stared at the frightening sculpture on the wall. He knew the Garuda god was watching him. Watching and waiting for him to relinquish the will to fight.

FEAR WAS THE FIRST emotion that struck Louisiana when she woke up. She lay very still on the pallet inside the cabin and tried to get her bearings. The movement of the boat disoriented her and it took several seconds for her to realize where she was.

She heard the voices of Gunner and Bruno just outside the cabin and she could see that it was morning. Propping up on one elbow, she watched them through the canvas opening. They were both now dressed in camouflage and they hovered over a large piece of paper, a map of some sort.

"Up in here," Gunner was saying.

"Route to border like this," said Bruno. His next words were garbled and tonal, words that Louisiana couldn't understand.

"If I had smuggled those rubies," Gunner murmured, "I'd route them through Burma."

"Yes. Tavoy or Moulmein, maybe."

Louisiana squeezed her eyes shut in an attempt to block the painful memory of sensations that rushed over her. The touch of his fingers on her skin, the feel of his warm mouth. Gunner's body against hers.

She had never felt so disgusted with herself in her life. She felt used. Why had she done it? She had allowed her own restless longings to distract her from the reason to be here. She had come here because her brother needed her. Ham was in trouble, in danger, maybe even...no, she wouldn't allow that final thought to penetrate. He was in some kind of serious trouble and last night she had forgotten about that—and about him. She had been lost in sensual pleasure, encompassed in a gratifying realm where she was safe and loved and where nothing but the impassioned stroke of a man's hands could touch her. Outside of that, nothing else had existed.

The sound of their voices penetrated her shroud of misery. The talk was of rubies. She had been worried about how Gunner fit into this picture all along. Ham had not mentioned rubies. He had not even specifically said that Gunner could help. He had merely mentioned his name. Yesterday she had wondered vaguely if he was responsible for Ham's disappearance. She still wondered. Instinct had warned her from the beginning that he was not a man to be trusted. He had been a mercenary soldier, so he was obviously not averse to barbarity and violence. What kinds of unspeakable deeds had he committed in the past? And what was he capable of now?

A finger of heat thrust through her. Last night his hands had not yielded violence. Intense passion, yes. And an erotic fever where he scorched her skin with each brush of his fingertips. Yes. But barbarity? Savagery? No.

She thought of the way he had reacted to Roxy's tears and pain. The simple stroke of his hand had revealed a strong sense of caring toward the girl. And last night, hadn't she felt more than just heat coming from him? Wasn't there tenderness in his touch and in his words, as well?

Still, he had used her fear and the primitive struggle of the moment to satisfy his own pressing need. She mustn't forget that. She mustn't assume that it was anything more than a flash of heat in the night.

She slid from the soft pallet Gunner had provided for her and straightened the clean clothes he had given her last night. She didn't like to depend on others for her needs; it made her feel captive and diminished.

She looked around the small cabin. It was packed with household goods, enamel plates and cooking pots, cups and utensils. The place was pared to the bare essentials. There wasn't a single homey touch. But then, it would be a little hard to imagine anyone wanting to make a home on this peeling barge with the likes of Bruno.

At the head of the pallet was one of the boxes they had loaded onto the boat from the dock last night. She glanced back to make sure they were still absorbed in their conversation, then she lifted the flap on the box. Her pulse began to race. Inside were the guns that Gunner and Bruno had used to blast away from Tak's men. And beneath those, the carton was crammed full of weapons. There were machine guns, rifles, guns with long scopes, strange-looking binoculars, stainless-steel daggers.

Her pounding heart felt trapped inside her chest. What was all this for? They had enough weapons here to equip a small army!

A deep growl reverberated behind her. Bruno's beefy hand grasped her wrist and her body jerked as he pulled her back. "No!" he shouted, his glowering face only inches from hers.

Gunner stooped under the canvas and Bruno, never releasing the pressure on her wrist, glanced back. "She was looking. In the box."

"Let her go."

Bruno stared at Gunner for one belligerent moment, then reluctantly released her.

Louisiana stepped back and grabbed her wrist, kneading the flesh with her other hand. She stared at Gunner and he at her. Tension arced between them. The air was saturated with the lingering moments of their night together. In those brief seconds of taut silence, every flaming touch was felt, every low murmur heard.

Gunner stepped up to her and stood less than a foot away. His gaze centered on her mouth, then lifted to her eyes. He glanced at the box and then back at her. "What were you doing, Louisiana?"

Anger swam to the surface. "Nothing to warrant an assault from your brute squad."

Gunner reached for her hand and examined her wrist. Bruno hadn't hurt her and he knew it. She knew it, too, but she wasn't going to let either of them off that easily.

Finding no injuries, Gunner let her hand go. "What were you looking for?"

"Breakfast."

His eyes locked with hers. "In there?"

"She knows much," Bruno growled. "I told you she bring trouble."

Gunner stared at her. "Are you going to be trouble, Louisiana?"

She glanced at the box and then back at him. "Is that how you help people do business in Thailand? Ditchdiggers from Timbuktu to Kalamazoo and all that?"

"Those weapons have nothing to do with you."

"And what about Ham?"

"I told you I'd find Ham."

"Yeah? Well, funny, I don't believe you."

Gunner looked back at Bruno and the ugly man grumbled, "Trouble. Bad thing to bother the sleeping gods." Then he quickly slipped under the canvas and moved to the stern. It was just past dawn, Louisiana realized, and the water glowed with a silvery, salmon hue. Boats unnoticed in the dark of night now clustered like schools of fish. There were sampans and fishing boats, some brightly painted, some with long tails kicking up a fan of water behind them. The engine revved louder and Louisiana felt the boat turn.

"Where is he going?" she asked suspiciously.

"He's moving out of the main channel," said Gunner. "Into a smaller canal."

"Why?"

"Here, we can be easily spotted in full daylight. We don't want that."

A new wave of panic struck her nerves. "You mean—you think those men are following us?"

"I would if I were them."

Louisiana crossed her arms, hugging them close to her body, wishing like mad that she could act as self-possessed as Gunner was. He stood there with that calm exterior so intact, so unflappable, without the least hint of a crack in the facade.

Jai yen, that's what he was. One cool heart.

Emotionally she was standing on a cliff's edge, and she had never felt so vulnerable in her life. He dangled temptations before her without effort, baiting her with nothing more than a look, a slight curve of his lips, a stance. But she had been raised with the stern Baptist heritage of resisting all kinds of temptations. And if the devil was indeed among us, then Gunner could very well be the incarnation.

"What did Bruno mean by all that gibberish—about the sleeping gods?"

Gunner had moved toward another box and pulled out a loaf of bread and some fruit. He tossed her something with a hard shell around it. "Native superstitions, that's all."

"About what?"

Gunner bit off a hunk of bread and chewed it, watching her roll the fruit between her hands. "About the discovery your brother made."

"What do you mean?"

"The people in this part of the world have many superstitions. Legends tell them that to disturb the treasures of the gods will bring endless rain upon one's house."

"You mean like the curse of the Egyptian pharaohs or something?"

"Something like that."

"But you don't believe that, do you?"

He hesitated. "I've lived here too long to discount certain beliefs." He stared through the cabin at the narrow canal down which they skimmed. "There are things about this place—enigmas and secrets that always remain obscure. Riddles that defy explanation."

She suppressed the unease that tingled along her spine. Looking at the fruit in her hands, she asked, "What is this?"

"*Mangkut.*" He took it from her and broke the hard red shell, revealing soft pulpy sections that oozed with juice.

She bit into it. With the back of her hand, she wiped the droplets of juice from her chin.

Bruno's call carried into the cabin. Gunner tore off a hunk of bread and handed it to Louisiana, then left to join Bruno at the controls. Louisiana, watching them from inside, saw Bruno point toward the right bank. She came out and stood beside them.

On the bank were houses on stilts with families bathing and brushing their teeth in the canals. Behind the houses were an endless sea of bamboo forests, teak groves and jungle vegetation, thick and green, with only an occasional spire from a temple peeking up over the high branches of coconut trees. Palm trees lined the banks, their branches hanging low against the water. Birds cackled and cawed, flitting from tree to tree.

Bruno pulled the motor up out of the water and the boat slowed to a crawl. He picked up a long pole and guided them toward the bank.

"What are we doing?" she asked, wondering if they were planning to put her off here in this strange isolated village.

Bruno scowled at her question, but concentrated on easing the boat through the reeds and grasses that poked from beneath the surface of the water.

"You didn't answer me," she said to Gunner. "What are we doing here?"

His eyes fastened on her, but it was several seconds before he spoke. "I want you to stay on the boat."

Her chin lifted in suspicion.

"I mean it, Louisiana," he growled. "Do what I tell you."

"And where are you going?"

He hesitated. "Just to see someone."

Her eyes narrowed, searching for the secret passage into his mind. Into his intentions.

"I'd like to find a ladies' room," she said.

Gunner looked momentarily at a loss.

"Trouble?" Bruno growled.

Gunner translated what she had said. They both stared at her as if she were some rare and exotic species.

"I'm real sorry," she snapped. "I'm not like you guys. I'm only human."

Bruno pulled the boat against the reedy bank and secured the line to a coconut tree. Some houses on stilts perched a couple of hundred yards down the bank. Gunner and Bruno both looked worried, but Gunner glanced at her and said in a reluctant voice, "I'll let you get out of the boat, but you're to do exactly as I say. Got that?"

"Loud and clear."

Grumbling to himself, he ducked beneath the canvas roof and came back with some socks and a pair of lace-up boots. "Put these on before you get out of the boat."

She peered over the edge at the stagnant water. Near the bank it looked like a half-thickened bowl of rice pudding.

"Didn't I see something like this in *African Queen*?" She looked up in time to see him slip a handgun into the waistband of his camouflage pants.

"Probably."

She looked away from the gun and kept her voice more light and even than she felt. "We're not going to run into any leeches, are we?"

"Just crocodiles. Ready?"

She tied the last bootlace, then stood. She was glad she didn't have to stay on the boat with the glowering Bruno. He looked as if he was just waiting for any opportunity to rip her apart.

Gunner climbed over the edge of the boat first, then helped her out. Leading the way, he thrashed through the thick tangle of bamboo stalks and palm fronds and tall grasses until he found a small clearing.

"This okay?"

She shrugged. "I suppose." It wasn't that she was bothered by having to deal with this outside. After all, she had grown up on four thousand acres. And when you were out playing with your oil wells on the southwest quarter of the southwest quarter of section ten, township eight, range three, you didn't dash back to the house every time nature gave a shout.

No, it was more that she wasn't used to all this tropical jungle stuff. She was used to flat, dry land, with a mesquite bush here and there, sagebrush rolling by with every breath of wind and the occasional rattle of an unwanted guest keeping you on your toes. The sounds above her right now were like something straight out of an old Tarzan movie.

Beyond that, she knew that Gunner was going to leave her here while he went off to visit someone. But who? And why?

"You wait here for me until I come back to get you," he commanded, extending his index finger for emphasis. "I mean it, Louisiana."

He spun around and thrashed back through the trees, coldly furious with himself at the mess he had made. This was not the way the scenario was supposed to unfold. He had too much at stake to let some damn female ruin it all. She was a problem; he'd sensed that from the beginning. But last night—dammit, there was no excuse for that! He had warned her that near-death experiences did that to him. He had warned her fair and square. Ham Bond's sister! Why the hell couldn't Ham have kept his mouth shut? There was no telling how much she knew or how much she had told others. No woman would be this persistent if she didn't know something about the plan. And if she did know, what was she up to? He could sense danger ahead, but he wasn't sure where the traps lay.

He brushed the flying insects from his face and tore through the thick fronds toward a small hut a little farther down the bank. The question was, what was he going to do with her now? If she were a soldier, he'd throw her in the clink for not following orders. Or better yet, he'd shoot her and be done with the whole mess.

He stopped and wiped his sleeve across his forehead. Who was he kidding if he thought he was immune to her? Every stroke of her fingers, the featherlight brush of her breath against his throat, the feel of her against him... Damn, Bruno was right. This woman was Trouble!

He climbed the steps of the small hut and stopped on the top stair. An older man, with graying temples, waited beside the door.

Gunner saluted. "Been a while, sir."

The man smiled. "What's time when you're my age?"

"You've heard what we're up against, sir?"

"Yep, sure have. You got enough men?"

"I think so."

"Think?"

Gunner smiled sheepishly. "I feel confident we have enough, sir."

"That's better," the older man said. "Now where are the men?"

"Some in Nakhon Pathom. Some back in Bangkok. We were unable to contact them all. That's why I'm here, sir."

"Okay, I'll get in touch with them. What are the orders?"

Gunner ran through the plan once more, looking for holes. "Ten o'clock tonight. At the bridge leading into Bo Phloi. We'll need a chopper and plenty of firepower. But the bird needs to wait down below in the valley. Bluey'll be flying it and he'll know to keep it covered."

"Okay," said the man. "Now what about—?" He stopped and stared past Gunner at something below.

Gunner spun around. A curse flew from his mouth.

Louisiana stared up at them. She had heard it all, and they knew it.

"Do we have a problem?" the older man murmured cautiously.

"I'll take care of it," mumbled Gunner. "You understand the plan?"

The man nodded and went back inside the hut, closing the screen behind him.

Gunner stood at the top of the stairs, glaring down at Louisiana, while an impotent fury billowed upward through his body.

"Well, well." She smirked. "Firepower and choppers. Those rubies must really be something."

She watched him come down the stairs very slowly, never taking his eyes off her. She was reeling from the conversation she had overheard. She knew now, beyond a shadow of a doubt, that Gunner was involved in something deadly. And not just him and Bruno, but others. Lots of others by the sound of it. She had to get away from him, but she didn't know how.

The space closed between them as he drew near, with that cold, implacable fury stamped on every plane of his face. She had to get away. He was dangerous. She had to save her brother—and herself—before it was too late.

She spun around to run, but his arm caught her around the waist. She struggled, but he tightened his grip and lifted her off the ground.

"Where are you going, Louisiana?" he whispered against her ear. "I thought you liked being with me." His teeth were clenched together, but the words were uttered like a seductive purr. "That's why you can't stay away, isn't it?" He squeezed tighter. "Isn't it? That's why you keep following me."

The warmth of his low breath against her neck made it difficult to think. "Let go of me!"

He loosened his hold and let her drop to her feet. But he retained a grasp on her arm. "Are you in some sort of hurry to get away from me?"

"You're a thief." She sneered. "I know it and I now know what your plans are."

"Do you, now?"

"That's right."

He pulled her closer. "And what are you going to do with your newfound knowledge?"

"Tell the proper authorities and then have them help me find my brother."

"And just who are the proper authorities, Louisiana?" His voice was dangerously low. "The minister of public works? Who?"

"I'll find the right person."

"How? You don't trust anyone, remember. So tell me, how are you going to know who is dangerous and who is not?"

She stared boldly into his eyes, but her heart felt as if it would thump its way out of her rib cage. "I know *you* are."

He paused while his eyes inched over her face, absorbing and detailing every frightened thought that tumbled through her mind. His voice, when he finally spoke, was like the primitive whisper of the steaming jungle around them, subtle and savage. "Yeah, Louisiana, you are right about that. I'm dangerous." He had closed the gap between them and she could feel the palpable heat of his body transferred to hers. "In fact, when I'm crossed, I might just be the most dangerous man alive."

Last night had been a chance encounter; he knew that and so did she. Still, his fingers burned where they lay against her arm and he suddenly wondered who was in more danger here—him or her.

"We've got to go," he forced himself to say, looking back at the boat.

Louisiana tried to free her arm, but had no success. "I'm not going with you any farther, Gunner."

He looked around at the few meager huts and the endless miles of impenetrable jungle that lay between here and anywhere. "You're going to Nakhon Pathom," he said. "With me."

"As your prisoner of war?" she snapped.

"If you want to look at it that way." Without letting go of her arm, he led her back down the soggy bank of the canal, toward the peeling boat, toward a surly Bruno and toward a very uncertain future.

Okay, Louisiana, calm down and think. Think about what you should do. Roxy had said that Tak was going to his farm to take care of the abbot. So they were going to the right place, anyway—she hoped. Nakhon Pathom was near Kanchanaburi, and that was near where the statue was found. That's where Tak had his rice farm. That's where they were headed. Okay, so that part was still on track. But once they got there, Gunner and Bruno were going to be searching for rubies. She would have to get away from them there. She would have to escape to find Ham on her own.

She stiffened her spine. That was what it all boiled down to in the end. Daddy Bond had been right on the mark. *You gotta milk your own duck,* he always said. *To have it done right, you've got to do it on your own.* Alone. That's the way it had been for Louisiana for a long time. She was alone. She was on her own. She had no one to depend upon but herself.

She stared at Gunner's back. She wished being alone weren't so tiring. If only she didn't feel as if something good and substantial was missing from her life.

It wasn't that she was frightened by the prospect of being by herself. She was used to that. She was used to

the almost overwhelming responsibility of walking in
her father's shoes. He hadn't raised her to need anyone. Still . . .

Walking behind Gunner now, she couldn't hide the
painful regret that he wasn't the man that a part of her
needed and had hoped he would be.

Drained from the heat and the exhausting emotional battle, Louisiana climbed back into the boat,
only to be confronted with the suspicion and con-
tempt of two men who had saved her life and, at the
same time, who posed a dark and shadowy threat that
descended over her like a shapeless, menacing cloud.

That sunny dome! those caves of ice!

Chapter Ten

A cone-shaped spire rose above the horizon, gleaming like burnished gold in the sunlight. From her spot in the front of the boat, Louisiana could see it rising up like a dragon from the deep. Morning rain had fallen intermittently and, though the clouds above them were still the color of ashes, in the distance the sky was a dazzling blue-white.

She might be a virtual prisoner on this boat, but she was not going to let them intimidate her into sitting in the dingy cabin. Bruno was coiling rope up front. Louisiana sat in the back, a few feet away from where Gunner was holding on to the steering arm.

"What is that thing in the distance?"

"Phra Pathom Chedi."

"Okay, if you say so."

He glanced at her. "It's the highest Buddhist monument in the world."

"So that's the town of Nakhon Pathom?"

"Yes."

"And that's where we're going to dock?"

He paused before answering. "That's right, but now I want you to listen to me." He stared at that soft angelic face, so incongruous with these harsh surroundings, and cursed his weakness around her. "Are you listening?"

"I'm listening."

"We expect trouble when we get there, and—"

"From Tak's men?"

"Yes, and when we're dealing with them, I don't want to be worried about you."

"Why would you be worried? I'd think you'd relish any chance to be rid of me."

His eyes fastened on her and he forced himself to speak with a detached calm he didn't feel. "I'd be worried that you'd get in our way."

"Ah."

"This isn't a game, Louisiana. Now I mean it. You're going to have to do exactly what I say."

The tension in his voice transferred to her and she lost the flippant tone. "You think—you think it will be like before? With the shooting and all?"

Gunner's eyes narrowed in thought on the cone-shaped spire. "I just know they'll be there."

Louisiana sat silent and thoughtful, working on various ideas for escaping Gunner and Bruno once they reached the dock. And escape them, she would. For she was convinced that they had no intention of finding her brother. And since that was what she had come halfway around the world to do, she was going to do it.

She looked over at Gunner a couple of times, wishing she didn't have these breathless, palpitating symptoms every time she was around him. She had many male cohorts in business. She'd had a personal relationship or two. She knew men who were friends, men who were adversaries, kind men, not-so-kind men. She had grown up in a man's world, and she had never had trouble relating to them. Conversations had always been easy and natural, never littered with meaningless drivel or awkward pauses. Louisiana Bond knew how to relate to men.

But this one...this one was so different. On the surface he appeared urbane and sophisticated, looking as if he would be more at home in front of a Harvard law class or overseeing a party of art patrons in a trendy London flat. And yet she had found him in an infamous barroom buried in the bowels of Bangkok. And she didn't even know his real name.

Beneath the polished physical appearance was a man who had fought wars in the swamps and jungles of the Asian world. He was a man who knew how to debilitate beefy bouncers with one blow, who packed enough ammunition to stock his own private army, who shot at men in the night with the sole intention of killing them. One who had warned her that he might be the most dangerous man alive.

As they drew nearer to Nakhon Pathom, Bruno and Gunner grew more silent and tense. Bruno took over the controls and Louisiana watched Gunner duck under the canvas and go straight for the box of weapons. She watched him grab the pistol he had earlier and jam a cartridge into the handgrip. He stuck it into the waistband of his camouflage pants. He pulled a dagger from the box, found a sheath and slipped that into his boot.

Louisiana tried to still the sudden tide of fear that washed over her. She tried to think of it as a movie or a book, not real. She was not really floating with two soldiers on a boat toward a remote region of Thailand where other men with guns were waiting for them. This was not a part of her world; therefore, she told herself, it was not real.

The land began to spread out, with the jungles receding behind them and fruit orchards and rice farms stretching beyond each side of the boat.

Bruno and Gunner conferred in garbled tones over the best route to take into the city.

"Near the museum," Gunner finally decided. "There's plenty of brush along the bank. And they might not expect us there."

Might not, Louisiana repeated to herself. But what if they did? "I need a gun," she blurted out and the two men turned to stare at her.

"What for?" asked Gunner.

"How about protection?" she snapped.

He smirked. "Honey, you just leave the protecting to us, okay?" He patted the gun at his waist. "These aren't toys."

They turned back to their plans and ignored her. Oh, that really irked her! She had been around guns all her life. Dammit, she could shoot a mole off a cottonmouth from the back of a bouncing pickup, so why didn't she just prove it?

She sat there, glaring at them, knowing that she wouldn't say anything because she thought that maybe, just maybe, they might be right. This wasn't a water moccasin hunt back on her Texas ranch. This was jungle warfare. No, she wasn't prepared for this.

Bruno eased the boat through a narrow channel and Gunner turned to Louisiana. He knelt down in front of her. His voice was full of command. "I want you to get that blanket now, take it into the cabin and cover up with it. I want you to stay there until I give you the signal to get up." He slowly and somewhat reluctantly laid his hand against her leg. His voice, when he spoke again, had lost its bellow of command. "Do it, Louisiana. Okay?"

"That blanket won't stop a bullet, Gunner."

"If they don't see you, they won't aim for you."

She stood, reached for the blanket and carried it into the cabin. Just ahead of them, the town rose along the banks of the river. They had taken a narrow canal, and the reeds beneath the water brushed against the sides of the boat.

Louisiana took one last glance at the town, then started to pull the cover over her. She stopped and looked outside. Gunner and Bruno knelt down and cut the engine. Staying low in the boat, they guided it through the thick brush. Louisiana watched them for a moment. They drew closer to the bank. She glanced at the box sitting a couple of feet away from her. She looked back at the two men. She didn't have time to weigh her decision. Her hand closed around the handle of a thick serrated knife. She pulled it out, glanced outside once again, then ducked beneath the cover.

The heat beneath it was overwhelming, but she could do nothing but lie there and listen to the sound of reeds scraping the sides of the boat as they glided through the thick brown water.

She heard Gunner come through the cabin and move to the front of the boat. She held her breath, hoping he wouldn't lift the cover and find her with the dagger.

The boat bumped against a large stump. Louisiana tried to block out the smell of the wet wool blanket. Gunner's and Bruno's voices were low and muffled. She hated waiting like this, waiting for disaster to strike. She didn't know when it would come or where.

She could only wait for the sounds of gunfire to split the air in two.

The boat slid and scraped against the bank and then jerked to a stop. She peeked from beneath the blanket and saw Gunner jump from the front and secure the line to a tree. He signaled to Bruno, who came through the cabin, reached into the box for a fat automatic rifle, then followed Gunner onto the bank.

They disappeared into the brush. Louisiana lay beneath the blanket, sweltering from the heat and listening to the rapid beat of her heart. She waited for the sound of their feet crunching through the brush. She waited for the sounds of their voices. She waited, but they didn't return.

Throwing the cover from her head, she sat up and looked outside. The boat rested against an overgrown bank. She could see no buildings, no houses, no other boats. There was nothing else around. She listened for any telltale sounds, but heard only the birds cackling in the trees above and the grasses tickling against the wood of the boat. She was alone.

She carefully set the blanket aside and stood. The boat rocked gently against its mooring place and Louisiana worked her way to the front. She stopped and listened again. Nothing. Where had Bruno and Gunner gone? Had they deserted her? Had they met with some accident in the jungle? Had they run into Tak's men? Where the hell was she supposed to go now?

All morning she had thought of little else except her escape from these two men and her strategies for finding her brother. But now that the opportunity was here, she was hesitant, unsure of the steps to take.

Still, she couldn't just wait around on the boat for someone to come get her. She had to take some action on her own, even if it was the wrong action.

She found a sheath for the dagger and stuck it down into the top of her boot the way Gunner had. From her purse, she took her passport and money. Those she slipped down into her pocket, and shoved her purse in a corner of the boat. Then, after climbing out, she picked her way through the thick brush, hoping to find a path of some sort.

She found one and hurried down it, hoping only that she was heading in the right direction. *But what was the right direction?* she wondered. She only knew she didn't want to go where any of Tak's men might be or where Gunner and Bruno were. Other than that, she had no idea where she was going.

She stopped and listened. There were voices just beyond the brush to her left, but she couldn't make them out. Was that Gunner? She just couldn't tell. She hunkered low and heard the sounds of men's footsteps crackling in the undergrowth. The voices drew closer, louder. They were speaking Thai.

So it wasn't Gunner and Bruno. She squatted down lower and squeezed into the thick covering of bamboo. Heavy boots went past her, within a few feet of her hiding place, heading down the path toward the boat. Her heart pounded so hard she was sure they would hear it and come back for her. She squeezed her eyes shut.

They passed by her, but it was several seconds before she could find her breath. She waited until her heart slowed a bit and then she stood. Her legs felt shaky, but she knew she couldn't stay here. She had to move on. She took a tentative step and then another.

Her breath came easier, her pulse slowed. It was okay now. They had gone in the other direction. Her path was clear.

She took a few more steps, then stopped, stifling a scream. A man stepped from the brush and stood before her, blocking the path. Her throat constricted. A fine sweat broke out. She stared, mesmerized, as a slow grin spread over his face. A million possibilities converged in her mind at once, a neon display of options and maneuvers and strategies. Yet not one of them could she put into effect. She was stunned, immobilized by fear. For in his hand was a knife, larger and more evil looking than the one she had hidden in her boot.

He took a step closer, and his eyes darted toward the brush, down which his friends had gone. She saw the split-second hesitation in him. He was trying to decide whether to call them back or to take care of her himself.

His indecision made hers for her. Not stopping to think of any consequences, Louisiana tore around him and down the path. Sticks cracked under his feet behind her and she heard his breath coming in thick fast pants as he ran after her. He hollered to the others, and she ran even faster. She didn't see the large branch until it was too late. Her foot caught and she stumbled. She took the brunt of the fall on her hands and rolled into the brush. She looked up and saw that the man was smiling. He knew he had won. He took a casual step toward her, in no hurry now that she was down.

Very slowly she slipped her right hand into the side of her boot and slid the dagger up along her calf. He stepped closer and bent forward to reach for her. She pulled the dagger from the sheath. He grasped her left arm and yanked her to her feet. She came up with the knife, swinging it out in front of her.

At the same moment, there was a loud crack of gunfire. The man groaned in pain, teetered forward, falling onto her. She screamed and jumped back, scraping her back on the bark of a tree. The man fell forward, facedown, and without another thought Louisiana tore off in a run.

She didn't look back. She didn't know if anyone was behind her or not. She heard the roar of fear in her ears and then she heard more shots. There were voices and the staccato sound of guns fired, but she didn't slow down. She ran for her life, away from the battle that was being fought behind her.

She came out in a small square. There were people all around selling their wares from small stalls in the marketplace to the groups of eager tourists. She struggled for her breath with her hand against her chest. She looked behind her, but no one was following. She looked down at her right hand and stared at the dagger. From its tip dripped a crimson line of blood. Her hand began to shake. She continued to stare at the blood, unable to accept what it signified. She had swung the knife toward the man, yes. And she had heard a painful groan come from his throat. But there had also been gunfire.

Her fingers sprang open and the knife dropped to the dirt. She continued to shake with a fear that had been delayed by shock. No, there was only a little blood. She would remember if she had stabbed him. No, she didn't do it. Still—it was human blood.

She had to get away from here! Leaving the offensive dagger behind, she sidled around the edge of the square, her eyes darting from face to face, searching for enemies, searching for danger. No one even noticed her. The market stalls were packed with wicker furniture, local produce, brass utensils, flowers and exotic pets. Around the square, there were signs of decaying temples and crumbling pagodas. She was amazed at the ordinariness of it all. Only a few yards back, she had been struggling for her life. Shots had been fired. Hadn't these people heard them? Weren't they aware of what she had gone through?

There was so much noise and confusion in the square, she finally realized, no one would notice anything.

She kept to the fringes of the crowd, wondering which way to go now. A railway station lay to her right. A couple of blocks north of it was a chapel and a golden image of a standing Buddha. The magnificent cone-shaped spire that she had seen from the boat rose over the town like a god.

She strode quickly over to a stall and bought a bottle of water. With shaking hands, she lifted it and took a long drink, trying to quiet the fear that rattled within her. They might come after her still, although she doubted that they would risk charging through the crowd to get her. If she could stay hidden amid the throng of tourists, she might be all right. She thought about the gunfire she had heard, wondering if Gunner might have been involved. But, no, she couldn't think about that right now. She wouldn't.

She glanced again at the statue of the standing Buddha. The one her brother had found had been jade. It had been discovered just north of here in Kanchanaburi. Someone in this town surely had to know something about the legend. Maybe here she could find someone to give a hint how to begin her search for Ham.

She glanced back once toward the thick jungle, then started in the direction of the standing Buddha, crossing an ornate bridge across a narrow canal. Here were more market stalls and mobile vendors selling every type of touristy trinket imaginable. There were refreshments and outdoor performances, giving the whole place the air of a carnival.

She walked on, not knowing which step was the right one to take, but sure that she had to find information and get away from that jungle.

A few feet away, a man was selling ice cream from his stall. She could hear him speaking pretty good English to the tourists, so Louisiana rushed over to him.

"You speak English." She sighed wearily.

He frowned at the way she looked. She was wearing baggy men's clothes and her hair was a mess. Her shirtsleeve was torn and she looked as if she had been crying. "You want *katit?*"

She looked back to see if anyone was following her. Her eyes cast around anxiously. "What—what did you say?"

"*Katit.* Ice cream. It's coconut. You look hungry."

"All right. I suppose," she said, realizing for the first time how hungry she really was. She had eaten so little in the past two days. And she didn't want to lose her strength. But she wasn't sure ice cream was the way to get it back.

She pulled some money from her pocket and held it out to him. He took the amount due and handed her a dish of the rich cream.

She ate the ice cream quickly and the man noticed the way her eyes kept roaming over the crowd, as if she felt that she was in some kind of danger. "You okay?" he asked, frowning at her.

She turned back to him, but it was a moment before her fear would let her focus her attention on him. "I need some information."

He shrugged. "Yes?"

"I'm trying to find out about the archaeological digs in this area and in Kanchanaburi. I need to find someone to talk to about them."

He listened closely, but shook his head. "Digs?"

"Yes, you know, ancient things—coins, statues, old cities, that sort of thing."

He puzzled a moment longer, then pulled out a brochure from the shelf beneath his counter. He opened it up and held it out to her as if this was what she wanted.

Louisiana stared glumly at the typical museum brochure. She was about to say "forget it" and walk away when she noticed in the lower corner a small photograph of an archaeological site. "This!" she said excitedly. "This is what I'm talking about. Does the museum have information about this?"

The man peered at the photograph. "Yes, yes, of course. You go to museum." He pointed to a map of the museum in the brochure. "You find woman. Old woman. Chusi Suwanrungsi." He jabbed a particular spot on the map. "You go talk to Khun Chusi." He pointed to the photograph again. "She know everything about this."

"Chusi," Louisiana repeated. "Thank you. I will. Uh—*khapkhun.*"

He folded his hands together at the chin. "*Mai pen rai*. You welcome."

Louisiana finished the ice cream and tossed the dish into a nearby trash can. She stared at the museum ahead, holding out a remnant of hope that here, finally, she might find some answers. If Tak wanted the hidden treasures, he would take Ham and Po to the place where Ham had found the Buddha. That was where Louisiana wanted to go. She only hoped that someone knew the way.

She glanced back at the impenetrable jungle. She swallowed a fleeting shaft of fear over the thought of what Gunner might do when he found out she had not stayed in the boat. When he learned that she, once again, had defied his orders.

> *It was an Abyssinian maid,*
> *And on her dulcimer she played,*
> *Singing of Mount Abora.*

Chapter Eleven

Gunner made it back to the boat before Bruno. With a painful grimace, he pressed his hand over his left upper arm where he had been shot. He could still hear shots behind him and could only hope that Bruno was at the firing end and not at the receiving.

Gunner climbed into the rocking boat. "Louisiana?" He ducked into the cabin. "Louisiana!" Yanking back the blanket, he stared in grim disbelief at the empty space. Her purse was shoved in a corner. He quickly bent down and unfastened the clasp, dumping the contents on the floor. Before he could examine everything, the boat tipped as someone climbed aboard. Gunner crouched down and cocked his gun.

"Damn." He let out a long relieved sigh when Bruno came into view.

"You are hit," Bruno said when he noticed the red stain on Gunner's shirt.

"Superficial."

"I have medicine." He ducked beneath the canvas roof to retrieve the supplies. "Where's woman?"

"I don't know. Dammit!" He pointed to her spilled purse. "Her money's gone. And so is her passport.

Where could she have gone! Tak's men didn't make it down here, did they?"

Bruno rummaged through the first-aid kit and shook his head. "I don't think so, but—"

"But what?"

Bruno hesitated as he processed the look on Gunner's face. "I did hear scream."

Gunner's reply was uttered through tight lips. "Hers?"

"I—I think—yes."

He took a deep breath, trying not to feel, trying only to think. That was what he had been trained to do. "She left the boat, dammit! I told her not to leave. I told her to stay put."

Bruno examined Gunner's arm, reassuring himself that there was no bullet buried inside. He opened a bottle of medicine and poured the fiery liquid into the wound. Gunner clamped his teeth shut and swallowed his pain.

"If she is alive," said Bruno, "and if they have her, she will cause much trouble for us."

If she is alive, echoed through Gunner's mind. "Yes," he managed to say between his clenched teeth. "Yes, she will."

"I think this is part of her plan," said Bruno. "I tell you she knows something—much more than she says to us. To you."

"She's not a collaborator," said Gunner, but he wasn't sure who he was trying to convince, Bruno or himself. He didn't really know for sure what she was up to. Every time he gave her a direct order, she disobeyed it. And while her courage was often foolhardy, it was still out of character for a woman. Women—at least the ones he had known—didn't fly across the world on a whim, then trek off alone into an unknown jungle in search of a missing brother. They would either get the police to handle it for them or stay home and grieve the loss. They didn't take this kind of initiative.

Of course, Louisiana Bond wasn't like any other woman he had known. He'd noticed that right off. Still, it was inconceivable that she would just take off like this. There were only two possibilities that he could imagine: one, she had been captured by Tak's men or, two, she'd had this as part of some plan all along, a plan designed to foil his own.

"Do we go find her?" asked Bruno as he put away the medicine.

Gunner stretched out his arm, forcing himself to move it as much as possible. "The rubies will probably leave the country tonight. We really shouldn't take the time to go searching for her." He stared at Bruno while the indecision volleyed back and forth in his mind. "Too much is at stake," he said, but the words sounded as much like a question as a statement of fact. "Still, if she is out to stop us, we've got to stop her first."

"If she is not with Tak, do you think she will go to Kwai?"

Gunner stared out at the narrow canal. "She is extremely resourceful. She seems able to find out exactly where to go next."

"Then we must go to that old man in the trees."

"Prayoon?"

Bruno nodded.

"I thought he was harmless."

"No one says no to Tak's money."

Gunner thought about it and finally nodded. "You're right. If we can keep a low profile, we can search here first, but if we don't find her within an hour, then we'll take the boat on to Kanchanaburi."

"You should have let me take care of her in beginning," grumbled Bruno. "You too soft."

Gunner thought about all the things Louisiana had done to him since he'd met her. His mind had lost the focus it needed to complete this job. And he didn't like the feelings and thoughts one little bit. "Women," he lamented.

"What you going to do?"

Exasperated, Gunner frowned at Bruno. "Well, dammit, we're going to rendezvous with the others, secure Tak's farm, his slaves, his jewels, and put the bastard out of commission. If we're real lucky, in the process Ham and his treasures will fall into our laps. Now what the hell did you think I was going to do!"

Bruno's face remained expressionless. "I mean, what do you do about the woman when you find her?"

Gunner glared out over the muddy water and wished Bruno knew him a little less well. He finally looked back at his friend and exhaled slowly. "I don't know. I wish to hell I did."

ONCE INSIDE the Nakhon Pathom museum, Louisiana asked a guard where she could find a woman named Chusi. Chusi Suwanrungsi's office, she was told, was located in the opposite corner of the building. She was directed down a narrow corridor and was told to turn right at the last junction.

She did and, halfway down the hallway, she heard a strange kind of music. It was different from the lilting tones of most Oriental music. It was an eerie sound, an ethereal and prismatic blend of strings and reeds that filled the air with mystery.

As she drew near, she heard voices speaking in Thai. The door to the office was open and, when Louisiana looked inside, she saw a tiny woman with silver hair and round glasses sitting on the floor of an office crammed with artifacts, ancient stone implements for grinding, shards of pottery and crude stone figures. There was no desk. On each of the woman's arms was a puppet. Louisiana paused, staring and listening. The voices she had heard from the hallway were not of several people, but only one. The old woman, talking in both a low, angry male tone and a higher-pitched feminine voice, was carrying on an animated conversation with her puppets.

She stopped talking and looked up at Louisiana, grinning mischievously. In flawless English, the old woman said, "We knew you would come. We have been waiting."

Louisiana glanced behind her to see if the woman was speaking to someone else. There was no one in the hallway. She couldn't stop the rise of icy bumps that crawled over her skin.

"You," said the woman, pointing a gnarled finger at her. "Come in. You have much to ask me."

In a daze, Louisiana stepped into the office. "Are— are you Chusi Suwanrungsi?"

The woman nodded. "I am. And you are?"

"Louisiana Bond."

The woman smiled. "Yes." She looked at the puppet on her right arm and spoke in Thai. When she turned back to Louisiana, she said, "They told me you were coming. I was not so sure."

Fear clamped around her rib cage as she thought of the men in the jungle with their guns and knives. "Who told you?"

"My puppets, of course."

Louisiana took a long look at the two puppets on the woman's arms. The one on the right had white bone-china hands and a beautiful face that protruded from a rich brocade robe, her white head topped by a golden headdress in the spired shape of a temple *chedi.*

The one on the left arm was also intricately carved and costumed. But this one was not beautiful. This one had the head of a monster and huge winglike fins that came off of its shoulders.

"The puppet theater is a dying art in my country, I am afraid," said the old woman, holding her puppets lovingly in her arms. "Video has taken over. And—" she shrugged, smiling "—I am old."

"You speak English very well," said Louisiana.

Chusi said something harsh in Thai to her puppets, then glared indignantly at Louisiana. "I took my undergraduate and graduate degrees at your MIT. I received my doctorate from Oxford. Now you should try to learn my language. That would be a change."

"Mrs., uh, Khun Chusi," Louisiana began, hoping the proper Thai salutation would soothe away any antagonism this very strange woman might feel toward her. "I was given your name by a man in the marketplace. He thought you might be able to answer some questions for me."

The old woman's eyes trailed over the tattered outfit Louisiana was wearing and her eyes narrowed in study on her face. "You have come a long way. You have been through much."

"Yes."

"You have the look of one who is lost." She smiled mysteriously. "But then you are never lost, are you?"

Louisiana was silent, unsure of how to respond. This woman acted as if she knew her. Or knew all about her. But that was absurd! They had just met. She needed time to get her information and then get the heck out of here. This place and this woman were very weird. "I'm interested in some of the archaeological digs in this area and around Kanchanaburi. I was told you know something about them."

"I know much about many things. What do you want to know?"

Louisiana wasn't sure how much to tell her. The more people who knew about the Buddha and the legend, the more dangerous it might be for Ham. She came farther into the room. "My brother is sort of a— an amateur archaeologist. He has done some digging in the area."

"The man from Bangkok...who is not who he says he is. I know him."

"Hamlin Bond? You know him?"

"Did I not just say that?" she retorted impatiently, then added, "So you are the one."

"The one?"

The thin smile was enigmatic. "Yes, the one. Let me ask *you* something. If you have questions about your brother's finds, why do you not ask him?"

Louisiana sighed, too weary and confused to hold back any more information. She desperately needed help wherever she could find it. "Khun Chusi, my brother is in trouble. I believe he is in terrible danger. And I think it is because of something he found near Kanchanaburi."

The little woman stared at her for a long moment, then indicated for Louisiana to sit on a pile of floor cushions. Louisiana did.

"Now tell me this story about Khun Hamlin," said Chusi after Louisiana was settled.

She did. She told her everything, about the statue her brother found, about the missing abbot, about Tak and his men wanting to find the legendary treasures. She told her all, leaving out only the part about Gunner and herself, the personal part, the part she still wasn't sure she even understood.

When she was finished, Chusi sat still for a very long time. She was staring trancelike at something on a shelf at the other side of the room, and it was several minutes before she moved her eyes back to Louisiana.

"Yes," she said slowly. "You are the one."

She glanced at the monster puppet on her left arm, speaking rapidly in Thai. The puppet was gesturing wildly with its arms, flinging them up and out and toward Louisiana while it chattered in Chusi's deeper malevolent voice. The female puppet interrupted, speaking in a high-pitched and frightened tone. Chusi turned to listen to it. When the chattering finally ceased, she fixed her eyes on a baffled Louisiana.

"My puppets are concerned about you." The angry monster flung its arms again and growled in words Louisiana couldn't understand. Chusi interpreted. "'This is not your kingdom,' he tells me. 'You do not belong here.'" The female puppet broke in, and when she finished speaking, Chusi said, "'Danger lurks around you,' they tell me. 'Fear consumes you.'"

Louisiana took in a deep dry breath, hoping to still the racing of her pulse. "I—I don't understand. Why are you saying these things?"

Chusi smiled. "I am only telling you what they tell me. Puppets see things. And they tell me you are in danger."

Talons of fear crept over Louisiana's skin as she stared at the old woman. "Will you help me, Khun Chusi? My brother is a good man. And—and I believe he is a seeker of truth."

"Truth often leads to danger," said Chusi.

In the past few days, Louisiana had learned all about truth and lies. She thought about last night on the boat in Gunner's arms. She thought about Ham, missing and perhaps hurt in the depths of this foreign land. Both lies and truths could lead one to inescapable danger. "Yes," she said quietly. "I have found that out."

Chusi stood slowly, taking care not to rush her joints. "When they are ready for me to stand, I will stand," she explained. Still holding the puppets on each arm, she walked over to the shelf on the other side of the tiny office. Louisiana could have stretched out both arms and touched each wall.

Chusi pulled the monster puppet from her hand and rummaged through a stack of papers that were piled a foot high on the shelf. When she retrieved the one she was looking for, she came back to the cushions. "That is the mark of a true archaeologist," she said. "You know—not one who seeks glory or fortune, but one who seeks the truth."

She squatted down carefully and spread a map out in front of Louisiana. "This is Kanchanaburi," she said and pointed to the small dot in the center. She swept her hand around the map. "All this is ancient civilizations. It used to be thought that the rice and bronze culture spread from China into Southeast Asia." She shook her head slowly. "Now we know that there is a real possibility that the flow was in the other direction. Here," she said, pointing to Kanchanaburi. "Here is where the cradle of civilization may have been."

"And that's why Ham knew to dig here?"

"He was not the first," she said impatiently. "There were many before him. There are references in ancient Indian chronicles about a fabled kingdom known as Suvarnabhumi and, because at that time Nakhon Pathom was much closer to the gulf, it is believed that this was the fabled kingdom."

Louisiana frowned down at the map. "But if this man Tak kidnapped Ham and Po and forced them to show him where the treasures are, how do I know where to begin looking for him? All I can assume is that they are all probably close to the site where Ham first found the statue."

The woman pointed her gnarled and bony finger, lowering it slowly to the map. She touched a spot straight north of Kanchanaburi. Her eyes lifted to meet Louisiana's and a slow grin spread across her face.

"Here is where the statue was found. Here is where I believe the treasures are buried. There are many caves that tunnel through the hills, many places to hide things. But you will never find the treasures, you know. The spirits will not let you."

"I don't care about treasures. I just want to find my brother and go home."

"What did you say?" Chusi asked the puppet on her right arm. She slipped the monster back onto her left. She spoke to the monster in Thai and he answered back. The beautiful one on the other hand joined in. Chusi looked over at Louisiana. "My puppets keep telling me that you remind them of the princess in the legend."

"What legend?"

"The one who came here to this fabled kingdom. Like you, she did not belong here and the king tried to tell her so. He warned her that he would kill her if she did not go away. She kept trying to find something that did not belong to her."

The puppets spoke again and Louisiana watched in curious silence and listened with rapt attention to words she could not understand.

"What happened to the princess, Chusi?"

The old woman listened to the monster's voice, then she fell silent and stared at Louisiana. "She was buried in a cave and left to die. Yes, the princess sat alone and lonely in the cold pit of death. Sat by a small pool of water, they tell me. All around her hung stark white skeletons. A slow drip of water fell from the ceiling above her into the tiny pool. She was very much alone."

A cold sweat broke out on Louisiana's hands, and she rubbed her palms against her legs. She didn't like listening to this kind of talk. It had nothing to do with her, so she shouldn't be afraid. But she was afraid. Everything about this woman and this place frightened her. She had the sudden and irrational urge to be wrapped in Gunner's arms. It was the only place, she realized now, that she had ever felt safe.

Her voice was insubstantial and too quiet. "And—did she die? Did the princess die there?"

"No," said Chusi. "She escaped."

"How?" cried Louisiana, unaware of how desperate she sounded.

The old woman shook her head. "I do not know. I will ask." She looked down first at the female puppet on her right hand and spoke, then turned to the monster. Her voice shifted from her own to that of each puppet before she once again stopped and looked at Louisiana. "A brave and honorable prince from her own kingdom saved her. He found the way into the cave. A passageway, it seems, that lay beneath the room where the princess was kept. At the hidden mouth of the passageway, a stone dropped into his hands. Water fell into his face. That is all I know."

Louisiana's breath fell and she felt something hot and stinging behind her eyes. "But, Chusi," she said very quietly, very sadly, "what if there is no brave and honorable prince?"

Chusi consulted with her puppets once more. "Then one must find the bravery and honor within one's self."

Louisiana stood and suddenly realized how very tired she was of all of this. She did not belong here and she wished more than anything that this were all a dream.

"Dreams can sometimes lead to truth, also," Chusi said and Louisiana's gaze jerked back to the woman's face. It was as if she could read her mind. As if she knew every thought that crossed her path. "The treasures of the hills," she added, "are for those who want them badly enough. Many have tried. All, so far, have failed."

"Are you trying to find the treasures, Khun Chusi?"

The old woman's eyes fastened on Louisiana. "I cannot go back into the hills. Ever."

"Why not?"

"I have been cursed."

Louisiana was too stunned to respond at first. Finally the word slid out. "Cursed?"

The mysterious smile did not leave Chusi's face. But her eyes narrowed in warning on Louisiana. "Spirits guard the treasures of the gods. The hill tribes know this. They worship the spirits of the wind, the rain and the river. You will see this in your journey. They offer all sorts of things to propitiate them—garlands, rice, fruit. Sometimes it works. For me it did not."

Louisiana tried not to roll her eyes. "Khun Chusi, you are an educated woman. You—you surely don't believe that the hills are ruled by spirits?"

"Ah, the jungle and the hills are inhabited by many evil monsters. Of course, these are countered by the benevolent female spirits who dwell in the trees. You will see them. You will hear them. My puppets hear them even from here."

Louisiana had to get away from here fast. This conversation and this woman made her terribly uneasy. "I—I don't suppose you know someone who would be willing to guide me into this area, do you?"

Chusi's trancelike stare ended and she nodded. She found a piece of paper and wrote down a name. "Prayoon Seu will help you."

"Prayoon. Is that a woman or a man?"

"Man. Woman. Spirit. You will see."

Louisiana sighed. "Where can I find him, uh, it?"

"You must take the train to Kanchanaburi, and then beyond to the River Kwai Bridge. From the lookout point for the bridge, there is a small path that will lead you to a house in the trees, on the banks of a *klong*. It is the only house down the road. There you will find Prayoon."

"The bridge on the River Kwai? Yes, I saw that on the tourist map. So—so I may tell him that you sent me?"

Chusi laid a gnarled hand on Louisiana's shoulders, a feather-light touch that sent shivers of apprehension down Louisiana's spine. "Prayoon will know why you are there."

And there were gardens bright
with sinuous rills,
Where blossomed many an incense-
bearing tree;
And here were forests ancient as the hills,
Enfolding sunny spots of greenery.

Chapter Twelve

Louisiana was exhausted, but sleep wouldn't come. It was a lazy train ride to Kanchanaburi, with milk stops at every sleepy village along the way, and she wished she could relax, even for a few moments. But her mind continued to race with all the unknowns that lay ahead of her and behind her. It was as if the trails left behind were piled with inconsistencies that would never lead her back to where she began. She was wandering, heading down paths that had no clearly marked signposts, leaving nothing to steer her back to the life she had known before.

She couldn't stop thinking about Gunner and those hours together in the cradle of the boat. Every remembrance of his touch caressed her mind, every tender murmured word came back to stroke her memory. How could she feel these things about a man whose soul was filled with larceny? How could she remember those little tender and kind moments when she knew that he had betrayed Ham and her?

She felt and remembered these things because she needed them so desperately in her life. It was not the first time that she had noticed a lack of something vital. She had felt its absence before. She had just never been able to discern what it was that was missing. Now—since Gunner—now she knew.

She stared out the train window and wondered how a life that had always had a strictly delineated purpose had somehow lost its reason and become as obscure as a Texas sky before a rainstorm. It had seemed simple enough at the time: Ham was in trouble and she had come to help. But somehow along the way she had found danger, spirits, thieves and a completely baffling relationship that she refused to call love, but acknowledged that it was as close as she'd ever come to it.

But that love had turned treacherous and she was left on her own once more. She would do things her way, the only way she knew how. So here she was on a slow-moving train, on her way to see a genderless creature in the woods who would know why she was there before she even said anything, and who would supposedly tell her where to go next. Life, she had learned the hard way, was anything but predictable.

She leaned back in the train seat and stared out the window, too exhausted to deal with any of it anymore.

The countryside became more primitive and untamed as the train rocked farther away from Nakhon Pathom. At first the land was wide and open, cut with winding streams that barely seemed to flow, and with green mountains looking cool and restful in the distance. Rice fields stretched on each side of the track, the shoots ripe and yellowing in the sun, collapsing with the weight of grain. Peasants stooped and squatted in the oozing paddies, cutting and gathering sheaves of grain and laying them in baskets. Old men in straw hats herded water buffalo down muddy streams. The pace of life was slow, set in rhythm to the weather.

A paradise, Gunner had called Thailand. Danger and deception were all that Louisiana had seen.

She closed her eyes and tried to picture the way he had looked when he and Bruno left the boat. It was only a few hours ago. A lifetime. She wondered if they had made it back. She wondered if they were glad to be rid of her or if Gunner was angry that she had disobeyed him once again. She wondered about him a lot, thinking of what might have been had they both been different people, meeting in a different place and time. She wondered, while the train carried her farther away from a fantasy that was not meant to be and toward a future reality that was, at best, uncertain.

In Kanchanaburi, she bought some bread and fruit, then changed to another train that would take her to the River Kwai. Even with the heat and the rains, the crowds still flocked to the famous bridge that linked the valley of Kwai Noi with that of Kwai Yai. She went directly to the lookout point and searched around for the path that Chusi had told her about. Her eyes swept over the line of bamboo several times before she spotted a tiny opening, no more than two feet wide. In the jungles of Thailand, Louisiana decided, that was enough to be called a path.

All along the river, people were having their evening baths. Children ran naked along the banks and splashed in the muddy water. The sun was low in the western sky, and the clumps of bamboo glowed in the red light.

Louisiana slipped away from a group of tourists who lingered on the lookout. She hesitated at the start of the trail. It was thick and overgrown and dark, revealing only snippets of light that angled through the branches. Unfamiliar sounds came from the mouth of the footpath, the shrieks of exotic birds, the chatter and squeak of thousands of insects, all vying for survival in the damp world from which they sprang.

Louisiana wondered if she really wanted to do this. It was insane. Yet over the past few hours, there had been perhaps too much speculation. She was Louisiana Bond. Billy Boone's daughter. A penchant for bold, decisive action—that was the trait she had inherited, the one so admired by stockholders of Bond Enterprises but feared by those in the path of dissolution. Self-analysis had no playing field. It was time, once again, for action.

Before forging ahead, she allowed one brief thought to land on an image of all those unfamiliar insects and snakes in the territory. But the minor distraction didn't deter her for long. It had never bothered her in the least to squash a bug that had the audacity to look her in the face, so if one dared to cross her path, she'd take care of it. That's what she'd do.

Still, she couldn't help but wonder what tactic one used to remove malevolent spirits from one's path. Daddy Bond hadn't covered that one, as he hadn't been big on spooks and goblins. And the only things he'd allowed to go bump in the night on their spread were the booms from his oil derricks.

With a deep breath, Louisiana started down the path, leaving behind the peace of the water and the security of the crowd. The huge stalks of bamboo arched menacingly over her and there were places where they had fallen, making the path virtually disappear. She wished now that she still had the dagger, just in case.

She didn't have to remind herself how isolated she was. No one even knew where she was. Mrs. Kruger thought she was in Bangkok at the Oriental Hotel. Gunner didn't have a clue where she was. So if she were to disappear now, no one—absolutely no one—would know where to begin a search. She would simply vanish, a statistic in the mist, without a trace.

She walked on, her heavy boots miring down once or twice in the ooze of the boggy furrow between the trees. The jungle smelled stagnant, like the *klongs*, a pungent mixture of spiced orchids and dead fish.

The sun dipped lower in the sky and, obliterated by the tangled mass of branches and leaves and vines, the jungle took on an eerie, surrealistic glow. The trees seemed to detach themselves from the surrounding forest, acquiring a life of their own. Louisiana thought of what Chusi had told her about the spirits who inhabited the jungles and the hills. Monsters, she had said. A chill ran over her flesh before she could rationalize the absurd notion away. Still . . . things were not the same here as they were in Texas. Life was very, very different. Even Gunner had warned her that things here were not always what they seemed.

Her eyes swept over the impenetrable jungle. A hot, wet wind rustled the leaves and made the bamboo stalks sway and screech. A mist began to slowly work its way through the trees, creeping over the track in front of her. Light could play tricks on you. Louisiana knew that. Light and shadow, dancing among the branches. Mists like ghosts, gray and hovering.

Louisiana looked back, but the head of the footpath had disappeared. The crowd of tourists and the security of life on the water were a dream left behind in the bright light. Here existed only mists and snarled underbrush . . . and spirits.

Chusi had said the benevolent female spirits lived in the trees. You could hear them, she had said. Louisiana halted in the track, listening for voices in the dusk, for the songs of spirits, but hearing only the incessant chirp of tiny insects.

Oh, this is ridiculous! she chided herself. What on earth would Daddy Bond say if he could see her now and read her thoughts? She could hear him scoffing from the grave.

Spirits in trees! Why, girl, that's as big a whopper as that flying armadillo you said you saw that time. She had been seven at the time and maybe it had been a dream, but the armadillo who flew had seemed so real to her then.

As real as spirits singing from the treetops.

The trail doglegged to the left. Vines interlaced across the path as if no one had been down this way for a long time. And yet this was the way Chusi had directed her. Louisiana pushed onward, praying that she would reach Prayoon's hut before it grew too dark to find her way.

After a while she came into a small clearing. The hut stood over a narrow runlet on tall stilts. The tiny canal held very little water, but the house perched on legs spoke of monsoonal flooding. A sampan was tied at the base of one of the wooden pilings, barely bobbing in the lazy water. The hut was isolated, alone, well hidden—the house of one who did not fear solitude and of one who did not invite guests.

Still, Chusi had told her to come. Had even told her that Prayoon would be expecting her. She shook her head, still dismissing that notion as absurd.

As she stepped closer, she saw that a small dark man was standing on the high porch, wearing a big straw hat that looked like a lampshade. In silence, he watched her approach. There was no sign of greeting, but there was also no sign of a weapon in his hand. Being an eternal optimist, Louisiana took that as a positive sign.

She raised her hand in greeting. *"Sawadi,"* she called up to him. "Are you Prayoon?"

He lifted his gnarled hand and placed a long bony index finger against his lips, silencing her. He climbed down the steps to the ground. When he walked up to her, she saw that he was no more than five feet tall at the most. He wore baggy black breeches and a long cotton tunic shirt. His face was tiny, with birdlike features. His nose was like a beak, his mouth small and curving downward on one side. His eyes, dark and moist, were a reflection of the dark jungle.

He lifted his hands in the prayerlike gesture of Thai greeting and slowly bowed.

Louisiana took that as a sign to speak. "I'm Louisiana B—"

His bony finger came up to his lips, silencing her once more. He walked away from her, toward a clump of bamboo, then turned back to see why she was not following him. She hurried to join him and he sat down, Indian-style, in the moist grass. He indicated for her to do the same.

She sat down and felt the moist ground seep through the thin cotton pants Gunner had loaned her. The ground and the little man smelled dank and old, both in need of sunlight and a good spraying of disinfectant.

Prayoon closed his eyes and clasped his hands in front of him. From deep inside him came a warm rich sound, a low hum that reverberated along his spine and through the ground, where it reached Louisiana. She stared at him, then glanced apprehensively at the jungle that surrounded them. It seemed to vibrate and pulsate with the sound from the tiny man's throat.

Louisiana shivered and rubbed her hand hard along her arm. A fear of the unknown bubbled up within her, and she had a sudden longing—an almost overwhelming ache—for home. She no longer wanted to be here. She wanted familiar surroundings and the security of the familiar. She didn't belong here. She no longer understood any of this. The people and the place had gone beyond the realm of her knowledge. And she wanted to go home.

Prayoon opened his eyes and stared at her as if he could read her thoughts. "Among them I walk. I speak to them. They hold out their hands to me."

Louisiana frowned. "Who do you speak to?"

Prayoon looked at the trees around them and he smiled. "For all time the words have been spoken. For all time the words of the god and of his sacred hills have been spoken."

Louisiana suppressed a new round of shivers, but swore she heard a lilting female voice singing from the tops of the trees above her.

Prayoon stood, reached for a large pack that hung on a nearby branch, slung it over his frail and stooped shoulders, then signaled for her to follow him. "From there we come."

Stupefied, Louisiana followed Prayoon down another twisted, snarled path, away from the house, away from a chance to turn back toward light and security. She followed like one who is sleepwalking, moving toward an unknown reality in the shadowed land of dreams. *From there we come.*

They walked until the sky was almost dark; all that was left of the light was a coral hush that settled over them like a cool sheet, relieving the heat of the day.

Prayoon said nothing more. He walked, and Louisiana followed him up higher into the mountains. The land leveled off and, stretching far and wide, were fields of rice and beans, mushrooms and flowers. The fields followed the slope of the terrain, climbing up the sides of the hills and sliding down into the valleys between each ridge. Here, there were three bamboo huts on poles. Beneath them wallowed pigs and ducks. On the porch of one, a woman was working in the dim light of day, working cloth beneath the needle of a treadle sewing machine. The men of the tiny village, wearing black jackets with brightly colored collars, stood silent and watchful as Prayoon and Louisiana passed through.

Just beyond the three huts was a much larger house, made of mud and bamboo and grass, and forming odd angles as it stretched across a corner of the field. Prayoon stopped and a new sound came from his throat, this one similar to the call of a barn owl.

The click of rifle bolts formed a choral backdrop as half a dozen men darted out from the darkened doorways of the house and from the huts behind them, encircling them with barrels aimed and pointed directly at them.

"Wh-what!" cried Louisiana, spinning around to stare openmouthed at the aggressors. Her heart began to pound upward toward her throat. She glanced at Prayoon. He walked to the edge of the circle of armed guards and passed through. No one bothered to stop him. They all stood stiff and alert, their attention and their guns still aimed at her.

Before the truth could fully settle upon her, another man came from the shadowed interiors of the house and stepped into the circle. He stood only a few feet away from her. He was short, but muscular, his features a mix of Chinese and Thai, his black jacket like those of the villagers, but also fringed with red tassels. But it was not his face or his clothes that Louisiana noticed for long. All of her attention was centered on the cowhide gun belt that was slung around his waist. The hide was tooled with a very special design, the work of a craftsman, the work of a man Louisiana had known all her life. For that gun belt, with its two side holsters, the one this man was now wearing, had been given to her brother by Daddy Bond on Ham's sixteenth birthday. It was his most prized possession.

Louisiana's eyes lifted to the man's face.

He smiled at her, the smile of a predator over its prey. "My name is Tak," he said. "I have been waiting for you."

She looked for Prayoon, but the evening mist had closed around him and whisked him away.

WITH HIS GUN CRADLED close to his chest and his back pressed against the wall, Gunner slowly opened the door of the bamboo house. He waited for a couple of seconds, then swung around, holding the gun out in front of him.

Bruno came around the corner of the porch and slipped into the hut behind Gunner.

They moved around the small room, examining everything.

"He hasn't been gone long," said Gunner, touching the still-warm tea in the cup on the table.

Bruno looked at his friend. "You think she is with him."

Gunner's jaw tightened. "All we can assume is that she is."

They went back outside and around the porch, climbing down the stairs to the level ground. Gunner walked around by the narrow canal. The boat was still tethered.

"Come!" Bruno called from behind the house. "This way."

Gunner veered around to the back. "What did you find?"

Bruno squatted low and pointed to the ground. "He went this way. And see—two sets of prints. The smaller one is the man's." He looked up at Gunner. "She was wearing your boots, so this one is hers."

Gunner's face was grim, his mouth drawn tight. He stared down the dark, narrow pathway, saying nothing.

Bruno's face, too, was clenched. "She is one of them." He shook his head. "I knew this. She has come to tell Prayoon of our plans. And she has reached him before us."

Gunner still stared down the path, but a frown creased his brow. "Or else—" His voice was quiet and questioning. "Or else, she has been led into a trap."

Bruno's head shot up. "If it is a trap. . ."

He didn't have to finish the thought. They both knew that if Louisiana had walked into one of Tak's traps, it would, without a doubt, be her last.

"No," said Bruno. "She is one of them."

"Yes," said Gunner, without the same conviction. "I'm sure you are right."

*Then reached the caverns measureless
to man,
And sank in tumult to a lifeless ocean*

Chapter Thirteen

Her eyes opened slowly, but she found herself wrapped in an emotional darkness. The tinny pelt of water dripping was the only thing she heard. She wanted to cry, but she wasn't sure there was anything to cry about. The place where she lay was cool and moist and she longed for the darkness to overtake her once more. But her mind sought daylight and familiarity and freedom from fear. It would not let her sink again into oblivion.

When her eyes first landed on Ham, she saw that he was lying facedown next to a shallow pool of water. A slim shaft of morning light fell from somewhere in the rocks above.

"Oh, my God!" she whispered in agony. "He's dead!"

She crawled over to him, laying her hand against his hair. His scalp was warm and soft. "Ham?" she ventured softly, tentatively.

He tried to lift his head.

"Ham, it's me. Louisiana."

He rolled over onto his back. The skin around his eyes was swollen and bruised. His shirt was wet and torn. "Are—are you really here?" he whispered weakly.

"Yes, Ham. I'm here." She ran her hand over his hair. "I'm here. Wh-what is it?" she asked when she saw him wince.

"My leg. It's broken."

"Where?"

"I'm not sure."

She surveyed his legs. His right one was swollen at the knee.

"Water?" he croaked. "Food?"

Tears streamed down her face and she brushed them away. "No, I don't have anything. I—I don't even know how I got here." She remembered hands grasping her arms. She remembered a pain-filled struggle, a fleeting glimpse of freedom as she tore free of her captors and then . . . then nothing more. "I can't believe you're alive," she whispered.

A small hum came from across the cave. Louisiana squinted her eyes, staring at the little bald man in the torn saffron robe seated against the far wall.

"Po?"

The man opened his eyes and focused on her. "You are the sister?"

"Yes."

The little man smiled. "He said you would come. I had my doubts."

Louisiana, fighting a sudden wave of depression, edged closer to Ham. She lifted his head and laid it in her lap. "I'm going to get us out of here, Ham. I'm going to find a way."

Ham offered only a tired smile and barely shook his head. "They've won, Louisie. It's over."

"No, it's not," she said between sobs. "We can't give up, Ham. Daddy did not raise us to be martyrs. He raised us to be fighters. That's what we are."

The walls of the cavern were moist and cold. Ham shivered in the circle of Louisiana's arms. As her eyes adjusted to the low light, she saw that the walls were adorned with earlier victims, a line of chained skeletons stretched around the perimeter of the cave. The corpses hanging there reminded her of the fate that could await them if they found no escape.

She thought of Gunner and his betrayal of Ham. She thought of Prayoon and Chusi and spirits in the night. She thought of Tak and his men waiting out there behind the trees for Gunner, Bruno and the rest of the fortune seekers. She wondered what Tak would do to Gunner when he caught him trying to steal the rubies. She thought about why she cared what happened to him. She didn't much like the answer that came to her.

She looked up again at that slim shaft of light that fell from the rocks above. There was an opening, a way out. If only she could get to it. *If only . . .*

THE CHOPPERS WHIRRED loudly as they dropped into the tiny clearing in the jungle, and the bamboo shuddered in the wake of the air stirred by the metal blades.

A dozen commandos carrying automatic rifles jumped from the helicopters and, stooping low, scrambled over to the edge of the forest where Gunner and several other soldiers waited.

The officer of the new group, a man called Bluey, saluted Gunner and said, "What does it look like, Major?"

Gunner hunkered down and cleared the twigs and leaves out of the path. With his finger in the mud, he began to draw Tak's compound, showing all the possible routes in and out. He had already found the farm and had memorized its layout.

"There are at least a dozen men guarding Tak's house. Then there are several other huts of sympathetic villagers. There are three huts of laborers guarded by soldiers."

"Slave laborers?" asked Bluey.

Gunner stood and nodded.

"Is that what this mission's all about, then— slaves?"

Gunner bummed a cigarette from him, flicked a match with his thumbnail and lit the tip. He hadn't smoked for a long time but, dammit, he needed one now. He inhaled deeply, trying to bring his thoughts into focus. What the hell was this mission all about, anyway? There were too many interlopers at the party, too many distractions he hadn't banked on. It was she who was tying him up in knots. Louisiana. He couldn't get rid of her. His mind was filled with the memory of her hands stroking his body and the soft sigh from her throat in the dark of the night. She was an irritant that confused him, made him distrust her and, at the same time, made him hunger for her like a starving man. He didn't want to think what Tak would do to her if he captured her, and he didn't trust her to keep her mouth shut about his and Bruno's plans.

Gunner took another drag from the cigarette and looked over the men watching him, waiting for his answer. He thought about Ham, the jade Buddha, Tak, slaves and the rubies. But his thoughts lingered the longest on the drenched and trembling woman who, beneath a mist-draped moon, had clung to him in search of protection and a few hours of tenderness.

He dropped the cigarette, ground it beneath the heel of his boot and glanced briefly at Bruno. He faced the troops waiting for his answer, then slowly and carefully explained exactly what they were going to do.

LOUISIANA PROPPED Ham against the wall. She crawled to the far side, forcing herself not to look at the skeletons. She touched the rock wall. It was solid. She moved around the perimeter, searching for a doorway. There was a narrow tunnel, but it was dark. "The way in and out must be down there," she said. "Down that tunnel."

Ham's voice was barely above a cracked whisper. "When you give up the fight, you'll find peace, Louisie."

"No way," she argued. "They're not going to get the best of me. We're going to find the way out."

Ham leaned his head against the wall and closed his eyes. Louisiana saw that he was too weak to offer much help. She came back over to him and scooped some water into her cupped hands, lifting it to his lips. He slowly sucked it in. She did it several times until he opened his eyes and offered her a weak smile.

"Shouldn't have sent it," he managed with great effort. "So wrong."

She sat back on her heels. "The classified, you mean? No, Ham, it wasn't wrong. I'm glad you did. If you hadn't sent it, I wouldn't be here to help you. You did the right thing."

His head fell forward and his eyes closed in pain and fatigue. "No," he could barely whisper. "Secret. Always been part of the deal." He was quiet for several long seconds while he labored for breath. "Only chance. Gunner."

She swallowed the painful lump in the back of her throat and forced the words out. "He's not the person you thought he was, Ham. He's—" She cleared her throat. "He's not a friend."

But Ham didn't hear her. He had already fallen back into pain-free unconsciousness.

Louisiana laid his head down gently on the hard floor of the cave. She scooped up some water in her hand and carried it over to Po. He sucked noisily at what little her cupped palm retained. She went back and got some more for him, refilling her hands several times.

"Are you hurt?" she asked.

He shook his head. "Only tired."

"I told Ham I'm going to get us out of here. I mean that, Po. We will not die here."

"Death brings no fear."

"Yeah?" she said. "Well, maybe not to you, but it scares the wits out of me." She looked across the cave. "That tunnel has to be the way. I'm going to see where it goes."

"There are many chambers in these caverns," said Po. "You may become lost."

She stared toward the dark narrow passageway. "I've been lost since the moment I landed in this country." She stood. "I'll be back. If Ham wakes up, tell him—tell him I will be back."

The little man nodded slowly, then closed his eyes and resumed the chant.

Before she completely lost her nerve, Louisiana decided to explore the tunnel a bit. She edged forward, forcing herself to ignore the orchard of bones that hung like a sidewalk butcher's rack after a buzzards' convention. She tried, as always, to discount the negative aspects of this situation, looking on it as a wildcatter the way Billy Boone might, as a summons to show one's mettle. *You're playing cards with the devil,* her daddy used to say, *and there ain't no limit.*

Her eyes jumped to a skeleton hanging askew. The limit, she supposed, was that kind of death. Not, she decided, a very good hand to be dealt.

Upon leaving the main room where Ham and Po were, the passageway turned abruptly left. Running her left hand along the damp wall, she followed it for ten paces. But at that point, it then forked in opposite directions. *You may become lost,* Po had said. Po was probably right. She turned back around and let her right hand lead her back to the chamber where she started.

She sat down beside Ham. Scooping some water in her hand, she rubbed it against his face.

His eyes opened and he tried to smile. "I know I shouldn't say this," he said, "but I'm glad you're here."

She laid her hand over his. "So am I, Ham. We belong together. We're family."

"Family," he murmured. "You found Gunner?"

Louisiana held back the pain even his name caused. "I found him."

A tiny spark of life flickered in his eyes. "Then we'll be okay."

"No, Ham," she said, hating to quench any fire within him, however small, but knowing that she had to let him know that they were on their own. "He won't be helping us. He's—he's against us."

Ham stared at her, his mind too racked with pain to fully comprehend what she was saying. "No, we just can't tell you, that's all."

"No, you don't understand. Gunner is not who he says he is. He's a thief. He's after some rubies and your Buddha statue, too."

Ham barely moved his head to one side. "Not the statue."

"Yes, Ham. I'm telling you. He's not going to help us."

Ham closed his eyes, too weary to argue. After a long pause, he mumbled, "He always thought I was a washout."

"Who, Ham? Who thought that?"

His voice was a frail whisper. "Daddy Bond."

"No!" she cried. "He didn't think that! He loved you." She smiled and lightly squeezed his arm. "He just didn't understand you very well, that's all."

He slowly turned his head to look at her. "Neither do you, Louisie," he whispered. "Gunner or me."

The hours dribbled by in the cavern, relentlessly long and drawn out, and yet it seemed to Louisiana that her life was speeding by as fast as prairie gossip. Oxygen was thin, clean water scarce, life sources trickling away, minute by minute. Lethargy, like a creeping paralysis, began to overtake her body. She stared at the pool of water, lifting her eyes to the source of the drip that filled it. There was that slim crack of light, but no way to reach it.

"No," she mumbled to herself. "Can't let this happen."

Ham opened his eyes and turned his head toward her. "You okay?"

"We've got to get out of here, Ham."

"Honey," he said, his words slurred, "I can barely move. And we don't have the tools needed to blast our way out."

"But they brought us in here, so we could go out the same way."

"These mountains are honeycombed with tunnels and caverns. Tak knows the way in and out," he added tiredly, "but, hell, I wouldn't know where to begin."

"Why do you suppose Tak didn't chain us to the wall like these other poor slobs?"

Ham moaned softly when he shifted his leg. "Probably hoped we'd search for an escape and fall into some other trap. How did you get here, anyway?"

She sighed. "It's a long story."

"'Bout all we've got is time. Gunner help you get this far?"

Louisiana glanced over at the sleeping abbot. "What do we do about Po? Is he hurt?"

Ham's gaze flicked to his friend. "He knows how to move beyond all this. All is passing. The Enlightened One said that. All is sorrow, all is unreal. Happiness is a state of mind."

Louisiana shook her head. "Well, I'll tell you straight out, darlin', that my happiness depends on getting the hell out of here."

"You don't want to talk about him, do you?"

"About who?"

"Gunner."

Exasperated with the turn of the conversation, she stared at the skeletons on the opposite wall, hoping to erase any thoughts of Gunner from her mind. "No, I don't."

"Something happen between you two?"

"I thought he might be someone I could depend on. I found out I was wrong." Daddy Bond had taught them not to trust people. She had slipped for a few brief moments and look what happened. "You can't depend on other people," she added in a mumble.

"You're not always right, you know," said Ham. "Neither was Daddy Bond."

Louisiana swung her startled gaze toward him, but he had leaned his head back against the wall and his eyes were closed. Still, he said quietly, "I think my sister finally met her match, that's what I think."

I don't want to think about him, she told herself. *Why can't I stop thinking about him?* It did no good to waste time wondering what it would have been like had he been a different person. She couldn't change the reality. And thinking about him now was not going to get them freed from this pit of death.

Frowning, she mumbled to herself, "I just can't figure it. Why did Chusi send me to that old man, just to have him turn me over to Tak? It just doesn't make sense."

"Chusi?"

"Yes, this old woman at the museum in Nakhon Pathom."

Ham nodded slowly. "Spirit Woman."

Louisiana waited for Ham to say more.

"That's what the locals call her," he continued with his eyes closed. "Spirit Woman."

"Why?" She reached over and touched Ham's arm. "I'm sorry, you're too tired to talk."

He opened his eyes. "My mouth's all I've got left that works." He tried to smile. "Better use it while I've still got it."

She reached over and kissed his bruised cheek. "Okay, so tell me why they call her Spirit Woman."

"She seems to know things. Ahead of time. Like a seer."

"Yeah," said Louisiana, "I know what you mean. It was like she knew who I was before I even told her."

"She show you her puppets?"

Louisiana suppressed a shiver as she remembered the disembodied voices filling the small room, telling her of legends, warning her of danger. "Yes, and they made me feel like I'd stepped into the Twilight Zone."

"She claims her puppets tell her the future," said Ham.

"Hmm," murmured Louisiana, still uncomfortable with the pictures her mind kept recreating. The eerie music, the strange but beautiful puppets, the things they spoke of to Chusi.

"But why did she show *me* the puppets?" Louisiana wondered aloud. "And why send me to Prayoon?"

She shook her head in bewilderment, searching for answers to questions that were based more in delusion than reality. "If she knows things—" she continued to think aloud "—maybe she knew that Prayoon's actions were the only way for me to find you. But those puppets..."

They talked of a princess buried alive. They talked of a brave and honorable prince who came to rescue her.

Louisiana closed her eyes, discouraged by the curtain of hopelessness that was gathering around her. She listened to the sounds of Ham's ragged breathing and of water dripping into the tiny pool in the center of the room. Drip. Drip.

She felt like the princess, alone, lonely, imprisoned by the evil king, awaiting a slow withering death.

Her eyes flew open.

Her heart began to pound.

She looked over at the tiny pool of water. She looked up at the source of the drip. "The pool of water," she mumbled and crawled over to it. She stared down into the shallow basin. *A stone dropped into his hands. Water fell onto his face.* He was below the princess. The prince had found a passageway below.

She ran her fingers around the edge and along the bottom, searching for rocks that could be moved. She lifted out several small rocks, uncovering a larger one in the center of the bottom. With both hands, she reached in and, bracing herself as best as she could, tried to move it. The weight of the water on top of the rock made it almost impossible to move. And yet...

She felt it budge.

"It moved!" she whispered to herself. "I know it did!"

She knew she couldn't lift it against the pressure of the water, but if she could just slide it a bit... She closed her eyes and grasped the edges of the rock, pulling with all her might. This time, it shifted several inches. Staring down into the pool, she watched the water circle and spin and drain through the slim opening in the floor. She tried to pull the rock farther, but it was too heavy. She was going to need help.

She looked back at Ham. He was staring at her, his mind too numb to fully understand what was happening.

"I don't believe it!" she whispered in awe, still staring at him. "Chusi—her puppets knew the way."

"What do you mean?"

"My God, Ham! I know how to get us out of here!"

GUNNER AND HIS MEN fortified themselves with a few tins of food and, while they made sure their weapons were clean and loaded, they went over the maneuver for the third time. It was dark, but not dark enough for Gunner. They would go in at ten-fifteen, not a minute before or after. That was the time when Tak would come in from his walk and settle quietly in his house. He would be alone then. Taking advantage of the element of surprise was the only way to attack.

"Someone's coming!" Bruno whispered harshly and everyone took a defensive position, guns cocked, hearts pounding, eyes and ears peeled for enemy attack.

Gunner heard the crack of sticks beneath feet. There was a low moan. Lying flat on his stomach, he held his handgun out in front of him, ready to fire at will.

Three figures swayed into the light of the camp, weaving like a trio of drunken sailors. Bluey and his men surrounded them and two of the figures dropped immediately to the ground, too drunk or tired to go on.

"It's the captain," Bruno said.

Gunner clambered to his feet and edged forward, moving to the circle. Crumpled on the ground was Ham and the abbot. Standing over them was Louisiana, ragged, panic-stricken and poised for flight.

"Hold your fire," commanded Bluey, and the men's weapons came down. He and a couple of his men bent down toward Ham.

"No!" cried Louisiana. "Don't touch him!"

She squatted down and tried to push the men away. Gunner reached down and, grasping her shoulders, pulled her up. "It's okay, Louisiana. They want to help." She spun away from him and watched helplessly as the men lifted Ham and Po and propped them against two trees.

She stared at Gunner, her mind grasping for a single strand of thought on which to cling. She felt relief that this was Gunner's camp and not Tak's, but she was dismayed that she had come so far, struggling to help Po and Ham out of the cavern and into the jungle, only to find themselves at the hands of another enemy—this one possibly more dangerous than the other.

She wanted to throw herself against him and tell him how glad she was that he was still alive, that he had not been killed in the jungle outside of Nakhon Pathom. But at the same time she wanted to scream her fury at him for allowing her brother to be imprisoned in that cave as long as he had been.

She wanted to feel his arms around her, and wanted him to take away the fears of being locked away in that tomb of death, a fear she knew would not go away for a long time.

She stared at him, inflamed by a riot of emotions she had never known before.

He stood little more than a foot away, braced against some invisible barrier. He stared at her torn clothes and dirt-smudged face, a probing stare of disbelief that slowly unwound into relief, then coiled back up into stone-hardened anger.

"Louisiana," he said, the word wrapped in transparent sound, colorless, flavorless, exposing no emotion or position.

Her mouth remained tightly clamped, stubbornly refusing to give to or receive anything from him. She forced herself to look over at Ham where he was propped against a tree, making herself remember what Gunner's treachery had done to him, reminding herself that Gunner was responsible for Ham's misery, as well as her own.

Gunner walked over and squatted before Ham, running his hands over the swollen knee. "You look like hell, Bond."

Ham tried to smile, but he was too weak. "Nah, never better."

Louisiana watched the friendly exchange and her fists curled into tight balls, her fingernails digging into the palms when she saw Gunner reach out and lay his hand on Ham's shoulder. "Glad to have you back, buddy," he said, as if he really meant it.

Louisiana wanted to rant and rail at both of them. *How could you be so blind!* she wanted to yell at Ham. *How can you be such a villain!* she wanted to scream at Gunner.

"No mission—" Ham coughed and sputtered. "None is secure without me."

Gunner squeezed Ham's shoulder again and said, "Guess this time we'll have to take our chances without you. You rest up. When this is over, we'll get you in for treatment."

Ham nodded weakly. "Just make sure that when it's over, you've won. I don't travel with losers."

Gunner smiled and stood. When he turned around, he was again faced with Louisiana's cold, blind fury. He stepped closer. "I've got a few things to say to you."

"I have nothing to say to you and I want to hear nothing from you."

All eyes in the camp jerked toward the furious tone. When Gunner saw that the men were watching them so closely, he said, "Not here." He grasped her arm and tried to lead her into the cover of the thick jungle.

"Let go of me!" she cried, jerking her arm free.

He grabbed her again, this time more tightly, and hauled her farther into the curtain of trees. He stopped and glared at her. "You left the boat. I specifically told you not to leave the boat."

Her words billowed out like an explosion. "You never intended on helping my brother. And this best-buddy act of yours doesn't fool me for a minute. You were going to let him die up there."

Gunner's eyes narrowed dangerously. "You don't know what you're talking about, Louisiana, so I suggest you keep your mouth shut before you say something you'll really regret."

"You bastard," she said, glaring at him with a hate that made her feel miserable and lonely. "I'll tell you what I regret. I regret that I ever allowed myself to feel anything for you. I regret that I let you touch me."

Before she could sidestep him, Gunner looped one arm around her waist and the other hand held the back of her head. His mouth covered hers and the flames inside of her threatened to engulf them both. When he tore his mouth away, his breath was ragged against her ear. "No, you don't regret it, Louisiana. You just won't admit how much you need someone. Someone like me."

She pushed at his chest and tried not to cry, but she felt the scalding wetness behind her eyes. "My brother may be too weak and hurt to see who you are," she said, angry with the truth in his words, refusing to admit that he was right. "But I'm not, Gunner."

"I was worried about you," he growled, his anger fueled by the sharp, knifelike jabs of desire boring into him. To feel her against him and to know her from memory alone was enough to drive him crazy. "I thought Tak had you."

Her chest heaved against him. His mouth was only inches from hers. His body was heavy against her, pressing into her. "He did have me," she said between clenched teeth, then felt the tears begin to fall. "This old man—he led me right to him. I thought— God, I thought Chusi was helping me. I thought—I don't know what I thought! No one around this damn place is who he says he is! What's the matter with this place, anyway!" She wriggled against him, trying to get free from the one person who embodied all the uncertainty and complexity of this land where she did not belong, where she was a stranger.

Gunner held her fast. "How did you get away from him—from Tak? How did you find Ham?"

She tried to counteract the tears by retaining anger in her voice. "He threw me in a cave with Ham and Po. He left us there to die. There were hundreds of skeletons." She shook away the tears. "But I saved him, Gunner. I did it without you. Despite you!"

His hands tightened their grip on her waist and head and he glared at her for a strained moment, his nerves as taut and cold as gunmetal. "Yeah," he finally snarled. "All alone, right, Louisiana?" He paused, stamping out the fires within himself. He lifted his weight away from her and stepped back. "Just the way you like it."

Without another word, he walked back to the others, leaving her alone.

Just the way she liked it.

*So twice five miles of fertile ground
With walls and towers were girdled round*

Chapter Fourteen

Louisiana sat next to Ham and Po. Her brother slept, but Po was awake and watching with renewed interest as the soldiers prepared to leave.

"I wonder what will become of Buddha statue," Po said quietly, somewhat sadly.

Gunner glanced over from the other side of the camp, but Louisiana purposely looked away, directing her attention toward the abbot. Lowering her voice, she whispered, "What happened to it?"

"Tak has it. It is in house."

"How do you know?"

"They take me there first. They want me to tell them secrets it has, but I tell them nothing. So they lead me up into the mountains and make me dig. Only when I collapse do they throw me into cave with your brother."

"And Tak kept the statue?"

The old abbot sighed. "Yes. I . . . I failed."

Louisiana glanced over at Gunner and his league of men who were preparing to storm the compound and make off with assorted treasures. Yes, the abbot was right. Soon the statue would be in Gunner's hands. And, being the fortune hunter that he was, he would find a way, she felt sure, to learn the secrets the Buddha possessed.

She leaned her head back against the tree and wondered why she should care. Why should any of this matter to her? Ham chose to believe in Gunner's friendship. He believed that by tomorrow everything would be back to normal. So why should she keep insisting that it wouldn't? As soon as she got Ham to a hospital, she could go home, get back to work, forget all about this place and these people. Why should she care where the statue ended up?

Because she did, that's why. Ham had found it. And Po had vowed to protect it. Now Gunner and his men were going to make off with it. It wasn't fair. Dammit, it just wasn't fair and something should be done about it. But what? And by whom?

She swung back to Po and the whispered questions tumbled from her mouth. "Where is Tak's house from here? How would I get there? In what room did you last see it? Was it sitting out in the open? Was it put up in a case?"

Startled by such a willful woman, Po answered the questions as best as he could remember. "But you cannot go there by yourself. These soldiers will get it for us. Ham tell me that they are here to help us."

"No!" she snapped angrily. "They aren't. They won't get it for you. They'll take it for themselves. And you mustn't say a word to them about this. Not a word. Promise me."

Without waiting for his answer, she glanced over to the spot where Gunner was talking to the other men. Now was her chance, while he wasn't looking. She turned back to Po and laid her hand on his shoulder. "Take care of my brother for me."

"He will not like this."

"No," she said, taking a long look at Ham. "Probably not."

And then she was gone. She slipped through the brush behind them and headed in the direction Po had indicated. She hoped that by the time Gunner noticed she was missing, she would be too far ahead for him to catch her. Tak's compound was less than a quarter mile away. After coming this far around the world, a quarter of a mile—even straight uphill—was, as Daddy Bond would say, chicken feed.

THEY HAD FIFTEEN MINUTES more to wait and then they would begin the maneuver. Gunner glanced back at his three charges and his pulse immediately jerked to life. *Okay,* he told himself, calmly, *don't panic. She's probably just back in the trees.* He waited, watching for her to return, but she didn't.

He scuttled over to Ham and Po. "Bond! Wake up, man! Where is she?"

Ham reluctantly opened his eyes and winced from renewed pain in his leg. "What?"

"Where is she?"

"Who?"

"Your sister. Louisiana."

Ham swiveled his head to the side, but saw only the old abbot. "I don't know."

Gunner turned to Po. "Where did she go?"

The abbot was sick and tired of all the harsh questions that were directed his way, so he stubbornly refused to answer.

"Dammit, Ham!" growled Gunner. "Talk to him. Find out what he knows."

Ham shifted to a more comfortable position and turned to Po. "Do you know where she went?"

"I am not to say."

Exasperated, Gunner said, "Look, she could be in danger."

After a thoughtful moment of hesitation, and only after Ham nodded his agreement to Gunner's assessment, did Po answer. "She goes to save the Buddha."

Gunner stared. "You're joking."

Ham was still looking at Po and weighing the abbot's response. "He's not joking, man."

Po looked from one to the other. "She said you not bring it to me, so she go to get it."

Gunner squeezed his eyes shut and pinched the bridge of his nose. "She thinks I'm a thief."

Ham slowly shook his head. "I think I remember her saying something like that when we were in the cave. I don't know—can't remember. Just remember she was mad enough to eat bees. You didn't tell her the—"

"No, I didn't tell her what we were doing." Gunner looked at Ham. "I didn't know for sure what you had told her. She claimed you were in the publishing business, so... well, I don't have to tell you how the rules play. Besides, Bruno had me convinced that she might be working against us. I don't know—maybe I wanted to be convinced of that." He sighed. "Easier that way, you know."

Ham's gaze narrowed on his friend. "You got something going with my little sister?"

Gunner's eyes locked with Ham's and then he let out a long, slow breath. "Something—yeah. But don't ask me what the hell it is."

Ham tried to shift his weight, but the pain was too much. "Yeah," he said between clenched teeth, "well, if it makes you feel any better, I think you messed with *her* heartbeat a bit, too."

Gunner looked off into the jungle, his eyes gravely following the line Louisiana would have taken to Tak's compound. "She sure doesn't take orders too well, does she?"

Ham's eyes closed. "Louisie?" He smiled. "No. Saddles her own horse—always has." He opened his eyes. "But then, she's always tried to live up to Billy Boone's reputation. That's the way he was." He shook his head. "It hasn't been all that easy for Louisie."

"What about you?"

"Me?" Ham scoffed. "Nah, I knew I could never fill his shoes, so I just didn't bother to try. Louisiana, though—she keeps trying." He stared pointedly at Gunner. "You going to make sure she doesn't ride off a cliff this time?"

Gunner checked his watch. He knew that Ham's tone masked a grave concern, one they both shared. They both knew Tak and what he was capable of. And they both knew that once they moved into his compound, anything could happen. They didn't want to think beyond that.

"I'll do my best. She's—" He shook his head. "She's just so damn difficult."

Ham offered a thin smile. "Yeah, well, my old man always said the right woman was worth plowin' through a stump for."

Gunner sat very still for a long moment, staring off into the dark jungle. Finally a slow smile spread across his face. He laid his hand on Ham's shoulder and said,

"Your old man was right. And I'd say, then, that it's time to plow."

He signaled to the men that it was time to move out.

WHEN LOUISIANA REACHED the tiny village beside the compound, she hid for a while in the cover of trees and weighed her chances of slipping past the guards. There were two soldiers sitting on a porch in the village, smoking and talking. Beyond them, she saw one standing at the doorway to Tak's house. She decided to stay on the fringes of the jungle and move sideways around the perimeter. That way she could avoid the two on the porch.

The guard at the house left the doorway and walked around the far end of the building. Louisiana took her chance and ran across the yard toward the door. It was unlocked and she slipped inside the house.

Tak's house, she quickly found, was laid out like the compound as a whole, in sections. A series of breezeways connected the sleeping quarters to the dining and kitchen area and to the offices for the center of operations. This was no small farm, she realized. This was a major agricultural concern.

The structure was similar to that of Gunner's house, with window openings covered only by shutters, with teak walls and furnishings and with bamboo awnings over wide porches that circled the house.

The architectural style was quite different from the low-slung hacienda style she was used to living in. Her house at home—the one she had grown up in—was meant to close out the dust storms, the hot winds off the prairie, the harsh elements of west Texas. But here, people brought the outside in and the inside out, living in ingenious harmony with the world around them.

It amazed her that she could feel restful in the house of a cold-blooded villain like Tak, a man who had tried to kill her several times. If she had allowed herself to think about him back in the camp, she probably wouldn't have chanced coming here alone. She didn't want to think about what he would do if he caught her in his house. Now was not the time for thought; it was too late for that. Now was the time for action.

There were no light switches in the house, but gas lanterns burned brightly throughout. She could hear the sound of the gas escaping through the fuel valves. She crept around the office first, making a cursory check for signs of the statue. Po said he last saw it in the dining room, but while she was here she might as well look, just in case it had been moved. He had also described the statue for her, so she knew pretty much what to look for.

There were several offices and she made a quick pass-through of each. When she left them, she slipped down the breezeway. It briefly entered her mind that it was very quiet. The only sounds were those of insects in the trees. Even the breeze through the bamboo had grown still. The air was hot and sticky again and her torn shirt stuck to the middle of her back.

Suddenly she heard someone cough. She fell back into the shadows. Footsteps went past, going on through the office where she had been and out the door into the night. She left the dark refuge and moved on down the corridor.

The bedroom was furnished with an expensive antique bed and armoire with gold filigree and ivory inlays. Chinese in origin and design, it was elaborate and probably very expensive. Of course, anyone who dealt in stolen rubies could probably afford the best of everything. Delicate vases lined the top of a dresser and a collection of small ivory elephants sat on the table by the bed. On the wall hung two large elephant tusks. Here was a man who took what he wanted, period.

But again there was no Buddha.

She moved into the next section of the house, exploring a small primitive kitchen with a long table lined with wooden bowls. There was a fire pit in the center, no modern stove, but on the floor sat a microwave, its superfluous electric cord still wound up and wrapped with a twist tie.

The dining room was the last room she entered, only because it was at the farthest end of the house. And there, she saw, Po was right. The Buddha was the first thing Louisiana's eyes landed on, for it sat in the middle of the rectangular teak dining table. She was amazed at how easy this had been. Sure, there had been a couple of soldiers roaming around. But no one had impeded her progress. And no one was here now to stop her. She had succeeded. Easily.

She tiptoed to the center of the room and reached for the Buddha. A soft muted green, it was cool and smooth to the touch. It was heavier than she had expected it to be, but she hauled it into her arms and turned to leave.

As she spun around, a cry formed in the base of her throat. The statue slipped and she just barely kept it from smashing to the floor. She clutched it against her chest and stared at the man in the doorway. Around his waist, she noted, he still wore the tooled gun belt that had belonged to Ham.

Tak smiled. "Fortune comes to my house once again. I am like Midas, it seems. First I have the ancient jade Buddha in my home, and now the wealthy Miss Bond has chosen to join me."

"That is the last choice I would make," she managed to say.

He went on, ignoring her. "I must say, I'm surprised that you managed to escape my cave. I underestimated you and your brother. It is a wonderful cave, though, isn't it? So ancient, so diabolical, so full of suffering and death. We all choose the way we die, did you know that Miss Bond? Whether we realize it or not, we choose. You have chosen not to die in that manner, but, alas, the next choice may not be any more pleasant."

"Lots of people know where I am, Tak," she said. "You won't get away with killing me."

He smiled. "Oh, you must be referring to that special-forces team waiting out there to lay siege to my fortress."

Louisiana's flinch gave away her surprise.

"Oh, of course I know about them," said Tak. "The American government has wanted me out of the way for a long time." He grinned mischievously. "I am a nuisance, you see."

Louisiana felt the blood drain from her face and neck as the notion settled on her brain. "Spe—cial forces?" Her mouth slammed shut. No. Gunner was a thief. Tak must be talking about something else, someone else.

"You should never have joined up with that man Gunner. He and your brother may think that they are serving their country, but they will die for it. And because you have decided to become one of them, you, too, will die."

A jackhammer shuddered inside her chest. No, he had it all wrong. She had it all wrong. Someone had it wrong! She thought he was a thief. She thought... And Ham? Ham was in publishing. Ham didn't work for the government.

Tak took a step toward her. She clutched the Buddha more tightly in her arms.

He took another step. She backed up, but bumped into the table.

When he reached her, he lifted his hand. Like the strike of a venomous snake, quick and sharp, his fingertips grazed her cheek.

She drew away from the touch, but there was nowhere for her to go.

"I know how Gunner and Bond work. Their teams always strike at dawn." His fingers moved into her hair. "But just in case they have chosen to surprise me, I have sent out men to take care of them first. Your American friends will not make it past the first river crossing alive. So you see, Miss Bond, we have lots of time."

GUNNER AND BLUEY DRAGGED themselves forward on their stomachs. With their rifles grasped firmly in their hands, they lay outside the kitchen window, pressing themselves into the dark ground. The others had taken up their positions throughout the compound, some forming a line along the perimeter, others establishing a base outside each building.

They slid themselves along the moist ground until they reached the door. Gunner rolled quickly through it and Bluey followed. They crouched down at the end of the counter, straining to hear the conversation coming from the room beyond. They heard Tak's voice.

"The village women," Tak was saying. "Well—let us just say I like American women better. I went to school in America, did you know that? Berkeley, California. No, American women are not too docile. That is good. I do not like docile women."

Gunner and Bluey exchanged a quick look. Gunner slipped around the end of the counter and edged toward the dining room.

Louisiana jerked away from Tak. She was still clutching the Buddha in her arms, and he laughed at her. "You like the feel of that in your arms, yes? It is cold and smooth and hard."

"You come near me and I'll drop it," she warned.

"Then you'll never know the secret."

Tak continued to smile. "That is jade, Miss Bond. It will only crack." The smile left his face. "But I suggest that you put it down on the table now. You will make me very angry if it is damaged in any way. You cannot escape me, you know. I have men within earshot. You can either stay with me or you can take your chances with them." He stepped closer and reached for her.

Gunner moved toward the door.

Louisiana held the statue out, as if to drop it.

"You won't do it, Miss Bond."

She hesitated, wondering if he was right. It was ancient, priceless. It was the very thing for which Ham had almost lost his life. Could she let it drop to the hard stone floor?

He took a step.

Yes. Dammit, she could. And she would.

From the periphery, she saw something move in the doorway. Her gaze swung toward the opening. Tak, too, turned to look. She saw Gunner, rifle raised. Tak reached for the gun in the gun belt. Louisiana raised her arms. "Don't try it, Tak," Gunner called. Tak yanked the weapon from the holster. She lifted the statue higher. Could she do it? There wasn't time to think. Another man appeared in the doorway. She had to do it. With a grimace for the anticipated result, she brought her arms down and the statue crashed against his scalp. There was a heavy resistance of colliding objects. There was a deep groan.

And then he fell.

The jade Buddha lay on the floor on its back, staring up at the woman who had dared to drop it.

Gunner rushed into the room and pressed the barrel of the rifle against the back of Tak's neck. He checked the inert man for a pulse.

Louisiana, realizing that she might very well have just killed a man, felt her knees turn to jelly.

"Bluey," Gunner whispered. "Come tie him up."

Bluey rushed over and pulled some rope from his belt. He tied Tak's wrists and ankles together.

Gunner looked up at Louisiana and couldn't suppress an irrational twinge of exasperation. Dammit, she didn't even wait to let him rescue her. She had to go and put Tak out of commission before he even got a chance. She was staring down at the statue and he suddenly realized how pale she was.

He stood and started to reach for her, but loud voices drew near. A shot rang out and Bluey scrambled through the doorway to find out who it was. Gunner grabbed Louisiana and brought her to the floor. He pushed her under the table only a fraction of a second before the shuttered window overlooking the courtyard exploded in a hundred pieces, sending splinters of wood raining over the room.

Gunner came up firing and all Louisiana could do was crouch beneath the table and cover her head.

"Stay put, Louisiana." He fired off another round, then knelt down beneath the table. "I mean it. Don't move. Don't even . . . oh, hell, I'm wasting my breath, aren't I?"

Before waiting for her answer, he slid out from the table and ran out into the courtyard amid a volley of shots that reverberated through the halls of the house.

This time, Louisiana didn't move. Not because Gunner told her to stay, but because she realized that she was scared to death. For the first time, it hit her. This was not a game. This was for real. Life and death. She could really die out here in the middle of the Thai jungle. She was not at home. Not safe and sound. This was all new. Dangerous. Deadly.

And despite the fact that she had lifted the Buddha high in her arms and brought it with a crash down on Tak's head, she knew that, in truth, Gunner was the one who had saved her. If he had not come in when he did, the situation would have been very different.

She sat huddled beneath the table, wondering about so many things, about misconceptions, about lies, about truth beneath a facade. Behind her she heard a whimper, the soft cry of a woman. She sat very still, listening, until she heard the sound again. It *was* a woman, crying. The sound came through the opening into a hallway.

She hesitated for only moment before crawling out from under the table. Shots rang out just outside the window and she heard the distinct shouts of men as they ran across the courtyard. She darted into the darkened hallway and crouched down low against the wall. Her lungs hurt and her chest felt as if it would explode from fear.

The sound came again and this time she knew it was from behind the door at the end of the hallway. She scooted along, keeping her back next to the wall. When she was across the door, she reached out and tried the knob. It was locked. The second she twisted the doorknob, the crying stopped. On each side of the door, the two women sat silent, hearts pounding. Finally Louisiana spoke in a low whisper.

"Hello?"

The soft cry this time was one of relief and joy. She began to talk, but the rapid-fire words were spoken in a language Louisiana could not interpret.

"I'm sorry," she said, glancing back to see if anyone could hear. "I don't understand what you're saying. But please... not so loud."

The woman kept babbling while Louisiana shushed her and frantically began to search the hallway for a key. She found one in a bowl that sat on a table a few yards away. Hurrying back to the door, she tried it, all the while panicked that someone would hear the woman's loud plea.

The key worked and the bolt clicked back. She opened the door and stood facing a short frail woman with a bruised tear-streaked face. She continued to speak urgently to Louisiana in words she couldn't understand.

"I'm sorry," Louisiana repeated in frustration. "I just don't know what you're saying."

The woman grabbed the key and a lantern, then grasped Louisiana's arm and pulled her down the hallway, away from the dining room and toward a door at the end of the hall.

"Wait!" Louisiana cried. She held up her hand, indicating the sign to wait, then tore loose from the woman and ran back down the hallway, darting into the dining room and grabbing the Buddha statue from the floor. She came back, holding it in her arms, and followed the woman out into the dark night and away from the house. Shouts could be heard behind them, but Louisiana didn't know if they came from Gunner and his soldiers or Tak's men.

She blindly followed the woman, who led her to a large hut in the grove of trees behind. Using the key, the woman then unlocked the front door. When she held the lantern out in front of them, Louisiana saw that the room was packed with men and women and children, all huddled in a dark corner of the room, abused, undernourished and very frightened.

The woman said something to them and, one by one, they slowly stood and moved toward the doorway, bewildered but doing what the woman urgently told them to do.

Louisiana stepped out of the doorway and they all filed through. Outside, they looked around for a moment as if they didn't know which way to go. The woman continued to speak rapidly and urgently to them and, in response, they each stooped down to gather up stones or sticks in their hands.

Louisiana stood there, clutching the statue in her hands, baffled by the sight before her. Who were these people? Were these the slaves Gunner had mentioned? If so, what were they planning to do now?

After gathering their stones, the woman led them all quietly down a path toward the main compound.

"No!" Louisiana called out, wanting to warn them about Tak's men and the gunfire and the danger. But they didn't understand her.

She followed them, keeping well back in the cover of the trees. At the edge of the compound, the woman yelled something and they all rushed out into the middle of the fray, yelling and throwing their stones and brandishing their sticks high in the air.

In mute shock, Louisiana watched as a couple of them were struck by bullets and fell to the ground. She pressed her hand over her mouth, holding in the screams. It was absolute chaos in the center of the compound. Several of Gunner's soldiers rushed over and grabbed the children, one in each arm, hauling them out of harm's way. A man with a stick was clubbing another soldier, but Louisiana didn't know whether he was Gunner's or Tak's.

She lost all track of time. She was watching a war movie in the darkened theater of her mind. Reality once again was an elusive thing, something she couldn't touch, something she could hide from in the safety of the bamboo forest.

Suddenly everything grew quiet. The only sounds she heard were those of the birds above her in the trees. In the distance of the compound, people moved in slow motion. The woman and her people walked as if in a dream toward the center of the courtyard. Soldiers, Gunner's men, walked slowly toward them, without threat, without sound.

She watched from the sidelines, at a loss for the first time in her life as to what she should do. She had the statue. She could go back to Ham and Po and they could get away. But then . . . Tak had made it sound as if Gunner and Ham were working for the American government, as if this was a sanctioned mission. Had she been wrong about Gunner? Had she perhaps done things that were harmful to this mission?

She stayed back, holding the statue, unsure of herself . . . not acting like a Bond at all. Acting, this time, like a woman who has suddenly glimpsed some hidden truth about herself and doesn't know what to do about it.

Her body tightened like fence wire when she felt the cold metal tip stab against her throat.

"Don't move" came the low harsh command from behind her. "Don't even breathe."

The air was trapped in her lungs and her blood turned to ice in her veins. "Wh—"

"Shh. Shut up." A man's arm came around her torso, holding her own arms and the Buddha trapped against her. "Now we're gonna get out of here. You and me. Real quietlike." He prodded the metal tip against her skin and she felt the sting when it pierced the skin. A tiny trickle of blood ran down her neck and onto the shirt Gunner had given her to wear. "Let's go."

He backed up and she moved with him, stumbling. But he held on to her tightly and dragged her back farther into the trees with him.

"You can have the Buddha," she whispered, amazed that her voice could sound so calm when her brain was squirming with almost paralyzing fear.

"You're my insurance," he growled against her ear, still dragging and pulling her deeper into the dark. "So just keep your mouth shut."

Something snapped in the trees behind them and her captor froze against her. He swung around, flinging her with him. His arm clamped more tightly around her, squeezing her until the breath was forced from her lungs and could not be refilled.

Two men jumped from the dark, their rifles cocked and aimed. Gunner and Bruno, Louisiana saw, stood ready to fire. To kill.

"Let her go," Gunner said, and his voice was like the crack of a whip in a darkened cellar. "Let her go and back up."

The blade lay as an icy band of threat against her throat and Louisiana couldn't stifle the soft whimper. "I'll kill her. I swear to God, I'll do it."

"What's that going to get you? You'll just die with her."

Louisiana stared at Gunner, wondering at his words. Would he let her die? Was this one of those standoffs between two stubborn animals, neither of whom would back down, both of whom were willing to carry it to the death?

Her captor was very quiet for a long moment. Then he said, "Okay, you can watch her die, then. Her blood's on your hands."

Louisiana felt the man shift behind her and his grip tightened on the handle of the blade. She squeezed her eyes shut, knowing she was going to die, knowing that nothing she had ever done or had ever inherited was going to keep her alive. Her pulse pounded beneath the tip of the blade. She felt sweat form along her lip line. She really was going to die right here in the middle of this murky foreign land. *Dear God,* she began to pray...

She felt the jerk of his body behind her and her eyes flew open. In the briefest of seconds before she fell forward, she saw Gunner stoop down to retrieve the rifle he had dropped to the ground. In that split second, she realized that he and Bruno had done what her captor said. They had dropped their weapons. Despite what he had said, Gunner had not been willing to see her die.

She hit the ground, the Buddha rock hard and painful beneath her stomach. The sprawling weight on top of her crushed her against the muddy ground. She couldn't breathe. Through one eye she saw the knife lying inches away from her head, its tip stuck in the soft wet dirt.

She felt pain, but she couldn't isolate the spot. She wondered if she was dying.

It seemed like forever, but only seconds later the heavy weight was removed from her body and hands reached out to lift her off the statue. Strong arms looped around her, holding her close. Though in shock, she recognized the warmth of his body before her eyes could clearly focus on his face.

She looked up and he pressed his mouth against her forehead. His eyes were closed and his heart pounded like a herd of elephants against her hands.

Slowly the tension subsided and Louisiana was able to make at least partial sense of what had happened. Behind her stood Bruno. He was standing in front of the woman Louisiana had rescued from the locked room. He was standing before her and very gently prying the heavy rock from her frozen fingers. The woman's eyes were wide, shocked at what she had done, her brain not yet ready to realize that, this time, she would not be punished.

Louisiana glanced down at the man on the ground. She recognized him as one of Tak's soldiers. One of his American soldiers. He lay lifeless on the soft ground. The back of his hair was wet and red.

She looked at Bruno and the woman, absorbing finally that her life had been spared because of what the three of them had done together. Gunner and Bruno had put down their guns, hoping that by making themselves defenseless, Louisiana might be saved. And the woman—this woman who Louisiana now realized had been a prisoner and slave of Tak—had somehow sneaked up from behind and hit the soldier on the back of the head with the rock. She had saved Louisiana's life—the life of a stranger.

Louisiana turned back to Gunner. That inscrutable mask of his was once again firmly in place, letting no emotion show, hiding behind the facade all that he might have had to offer if only...if only she had been willing to see the truth.

In a rare moment of self-pity, Louisiana began to cry.

SEVERAL SOLDIERS CARRIED the crates of rubies to the waiting helicopter. Some of the refugee slaves had also boarded the chopper, while others would have to wait for another one to come and pick them up.

"They thought they were being led to freedom," one of the soldiers said to another. He shook his head. "Out of the killing fields and into Tak's fields. Some freedom."

Bruno and the Cambodian woman who had killed Tak's soldier stood aside from the others, talking softly to each other. Louisiana, sitting in mute shock on the ground a few feet away, watched in wonder as Bruno reached over and laid a gentle hand against the woman's face.

Gunner carried a box toward the chopper, not even looking at Louisiana. She had tried several times to talk to him, but each time he had to hurry away to help one of his men do something.

In the short hours it took to organize the rubies and the refugees, Ham had filled Louisiana in on the truth.

"I thought he was after the jewels," she told Ham. "And the statue." She shook her head. "Why didn't he tell me the truth?"

He shrugged. "Part of the package, kiddo. Secrecy in this job is everything."

"But you, too, Ham? Military intelligence? Daddy Bond never knew."

Ham shook his head and said sadly, "No. Sometimes I wish I had told him. Maybe things would have…" He let the thought trail off into the dark mist. "Well, now you know, anyway."

"How long have you and Gunner been doing this, working for the government?"

"A long time. Sometimes it feels like forever."

"So you knew about the Cambodian refugees being used as slaves. And you knew that Tak was smuggling rubies out of the country."

Ham nodded tiredly. "Yes. Unfortunately he also found out about the statue I discovered. He wanted me and I wanted him."

"But why did the U.S. government want to get involved in the smuggling of rubies and slaves?"

"It was more than that, Louisie. Tak's a minister with the Thai government. He carries lots of weight in certain circles. The U.S. wants Cambodia to stabilize. The Pol Pot regime left the country shattered. We're trying to help them rebuild and Tak was undermining that."

"Because he could profit from its chaos?"

"That's right."

"What about the magazine, Ham? Was that all a front?"

He nodded again and explained how it worked. As he talked, she realized that her insistent questions in his office that day had made them uneasy. And rather than take a chance on telling her something she shouldn't know, they had just closed down the operation.

"There was a woman, Ham, a British woman in Bangkok."

"You mean Victoria?"

Louisiana paused, not sure she wanted to know the truth if the truth revealed a personal relationship between Gunner and Victoria. "Yes."

"She's with the British government. They're working with us on this."

"And—and she and Gunner?" she asked reluctantly.

Ham studied Louisiana curiously. "You've fallen for him, haven't you?"

Louisiana's lips tightened. "You make it sound frivolous."

Ham's smile was weak and tired. "You've never been frivolous in your life, kid. That's my speciality, remember?"

"What about her, Ham? What about Victoria?"

"Nothing to worry about there, Louisiana. Victoria's been married three times and isn't about to settle for one man ever again. Gunner's impervious to her charms."

She didn't realize she had been holding her breath until it left her in a loud sigh. She glanced over at Gunner. He loaded a box onto the helicopter. When he caught her looking at him, he didn't smile. He turned around and went back to work.

"Sometimes," she said to Ham, "I guess the truth can come too late."

When the chopper was loaded, Louisiana, Ham and Po climbed aboard. Gunner came up to see them off. He handed Ham the gun belt Tak had been wearing. "See you in town, man."

"Amazing this thing went off so well without me," mused Ham.

Gunner grinned. "Amazing."

"Next mission," said Ham, "you might not be so lucky."

"Probably not." He nodded goodbye to Po, then let his eyes land on Louisiana.

She stared at him. It was the first time she had known the pain of losing something you needed this much. "I was wrong, Gunner," she said in a soft voice.

He swung away from the opening, then stopped, hesitating. He heaved a deep sigh and turned back. "Yeah, darlin', you were. And Billy Boone Bond was wrong, too."

She felt her throat constrict. "How's that?"

He paused, then said, "At some point in your life, Louisiana, you've got to trust somebody."

She stared at his back as he walked away. The blades began to turn, whirring fast and loud, and the helicopter lifted, hovering for a few seconds before it rose into the early-dawn mist, clearing the treetops on its route back to Bangkok.

For he on honey-dew hath fed,
And drunk the milk of Paradise.

Chapter Fifteen

The cool morning breeze stirred her hair as she stood on Gunner's veranda for the last time. His back was to her, his hands resting on the railing, and he stared out over the muddy *klong* that had such a hold on his life. He did not know she was standing behind him, watching him. Soon-Ni had let her in. Now that she was here, she knew there was a big part of her that wanted to stay.

"I came to tell you goodbye."

Gunner swung around slowly and stared at her. His expression was closed, controlled. She hadn't trusted him. And he hadn't trusted her. It was something neither of them could put aside.

"Ham gave me directions here," she said.

"So he's out of the hospital."

"Yes. He went back to his apartment this morning—or, at least, what's left of his apartment."

Gunner's eyes swept over her, absorbing all the parts of her that had already become a part of him. "You're leaving Thailand."

"Yes."

He nodded slowly, a gesture of acceptance. "Well, I guess corporate America will be glad to have you back."

The thought of it made her uncommonly tired. She tried valiantly to keep her tone light. "Actually, I wasn't missed half as much as I thought I'd be."

The tone did nothing to lighten the mood between them. She stepped up beside him and looked out over the lush garden, the canal and the fields beyond. "Ham told me everything, Gunner."

His face, she noted when she glanced his way, was still expressionless, a trait of the trade, she supposed. *Jai yen.* One cool heart. His response was a simple, "Did he?"

"Yes. He told me that you both work for the U.S. for the state department or some such."

A sigh slipped from between his lips and Louisiana could almost have sworn that it was one of relief. That obstacle, at least, had been removed between them. But there were others, she knew, that still lay heavy and solid, not easily moved.

"He told me that Tak was in the way of Cambodia's stabilization process. The U.S. wanted him out. It was your job to see that it was done."

He leaned back against the railing. "That's right."

"Why didn't you tell me, Gunner?"

"Company policy, Louisiana. I had no choice."

"That's not true, sugar. You had a choice."

He paused, then smiled, but it was thin and battle weary. "Yeah, you're right, I did." He frowned. "I've lived my life a certain way."

"In secrecy, you mean."

He shrugged. "Yeah, part of it. It's the game I chose to play."

Louisiana looked back over the filthy water. A group of children splashed their naked bodies and dived down beneath the surface to retrieve a glass bottle. "Even Daddy Bond didn't know," she said, as much to herself as to Gunner. "I wish Ham would have told him."

"You think it would have made a difference in their relationship?"

She hesitated, then sighed. "I know it would have made a difference in ours, Gunner." She looked at him. "Yours and mine."

His response was slow and measured. "Maybe."

"I thought you were a thief," she said. "I thought you had betrayed Ham . . . and me."

He nodded. "I know you did."

"And Bruno," she said, shaking her head. "My gosh, you could have told me about Bruno! That he'd lost his wife."

"Would it have made any difference?"

"Gunner, I thought he was the Grim Reaper or something. He never smiled. He constantly glared at me as if all the ills of the world were entirely my fault, and as if he'd be more than happy to put me out of everyone's misery." She sighed and shook her head. "Ham said you helped him look for his wife. Is that true?"

"Yes."

"What happened to her?"

"They lived in Phnom Penh. Under the Khmer Rouge, they were considered part of the New People, enemies of the government. They were forced to leave the city and they were separated." He looked back over the *klong* and said, "His wife and baby girl were sent to a village in the northwest and Bruno was sent to a camp in the south to work on irrigation ditches. It was '78 when he escaped. I met him shortly after that when he was in one of the refugee camps."

"And did you find her? His wife?"

"She was led with a group of other refugees across the border. Like those guys, those coyotes who work your border with Mexico, someone here promised the refugees freedom, but ended up enslaving them. We found out through government records that she and her little girl died working some man's rice field."

Louisiana's eyes closed and she said softly, "Just like all those slaves Tak had. And that woman who helped me—she must have been like Bruno's wife."

Gunner nodded. "Her story is equally brutal."

"What will happen to her now?"

Gunner's expression softened. "Bruno took her to his boat." He smiled, and this time it seemed genuine. "Stay tuned for further developments."

Louisiana shook her head in wonder. "I didn't realize that beneath that grim exterior of his, he was really a tortured man."

The smile faded. "I tried to tell you not to be deceived by what's on the surface."

She placed both hands on the railing and stared down into muddy water. "I'm a surface kind of person, Gunner." She looked back at him. "I need open spaces, big sunsets, cool dry evening breezes. Here, everything is so—so convoluted, so shadowy and mysterious. I need things that are practical and understandable and clearly defined."

He stared at her, knowing that, if she stayed, he would never tire of looking at her. Just looking. "I know that, Louisiana."

"I mean—" She sighed. "I know so little about you. I don't even know your name."

For a long moment, he stared at her. Then, making a decision, he leaned toward her. She heard the bamboo whisper above her, felt the breeze lift the hair at the back of her neck. He leaned closer and her breath caught. She felt pulled, drawn into something hot and mysterious. She felt his breath against her ear, his voice low and tantalizing.

She wanted to fall into the depths of that voice, to feel it around her and a part of her. And yet the words startled her into disbelief. She turned her head slowly to look at him, to see if he was lying to her. When she decided he wasn't, she couldn't suppress the giggle. "Sugar, you're not kidding, are you?"

He grinned back at her. "Nope."

She started to say something, but a laugh bubbled up instead. "I—" She giggled again. "I think I'll just stick with Gunner, if you don't mind."

His hands came up to her waist and he pulled her close. His smile had given his mouth a softness and accessibility. "I'd like it if you would," he whispered invitingly.

His words fell like the soft breeze against her face and, inside, her body tightened with needs she now had no trouble defining. It was so tempting. She desperately wanted to allow herself to have this, to know this happiness. And yet...her eyes closed briefly, then opened again. "There are just so many secrets here, Gunner," she said quietly. "Between us. In this place. I'm not used to searching for hidden truths and deeper meanings."

His hands slipped around to her lower back, pulling her up tight against him. "I don't think you have to search too far for the truth about us. It's clear, Louisiana."

Yes. It was that, all right. She knew what she wanted. And it would be easy to give in to it. And yet there were other considerations. Weren't there? There had to be. This kind of thing didn't happen to her. This kind of man didn't come into her life. "I guess," she said slowly, carefully, "I'm just not sure if I can accept this right now."

"*This,* Louisiana? What do you mean by *this?*"

She swallowed. "Us, Gunner."

And then his mouth touched hers, a kiss that was natural and inviting, like toast and coffee on a Saturday morning, like warm hay, fresh cut and piled high under a late-summer sun, waiting in the field to be baled. Like lovers, strolling hand in hand down a dirt lane.

Like lovers.

Like Gunner and her.

He looked down into her face and smiled very gently. The smile of one who cares. "You've paid your debt to your father, Louisiana. You don't owe him your entire life."

But she did, didn't she? She was the daughter of a stripper. She was the pretender to the throne. She owed him everything.

"Maybe not," she said and disengaged herself from his arms. "But that's something I've got to work on, Gunner."

"In Texas?"

"Yes. In Texas."

Reluctantly he let her go and watched her walk away from him.

"I'm glad I got to know you, Louisiana."

She stopped with her back to him and closed her eyes. She had to keep walking. She had to go. Now. Before she decided to stay forever. She looked back. "You, too, sugar."

Could I revive within me
Her symphony and song,
To such a deep delight 'twould win me

Epilogue

Steam rose from the jungle floor as the two men moved through the dense teak forest. They had been walking since early morning and now they had reached a clearing and it was time for one of them to stop.

"Are you sure you don't want me to go on with you, Po?"

The abbot nodded, looking down at the cast on Ham's leg. "You have done your part. More than your part. I know it has not been easy for you to walk so far on your hurt leg."

"I owe you everything, Po."

"No. God has given you everything."

Ham nodded slowly. "I'll be waiting for you here."

"Yes."

"And then I'll be going with you to the monastery."

"As you wish."

Ham looked down at the statue clutched in the abbot's arms. "You are positive this is what needs to be done?"

Po stared down into the valley below them. "It is best this way."

Ham nodded, knowing it was the truth. "I know."

"The greed of man is a terrible thing."

"Even if you bury the statue, someone will find it someday. You know that, don't you?"

"Yes, I know. But maybe that someone will be wiser than you and I."

Ham waited in the clearing, watching while Po climbed down the mountain, watched until he disappeared below the mists.

When the abbot made it back up to where Ham waited, the two of them picked their way slowly and carefully back down through the jungle to the village of Kanchanaburi below.

Above them, buried in the tangled jungle, beneath a mask of steam, the jade Buddha lay under the moist valley floor. Waiting. Waiting once again for its secret to be revealed.

THE COMPUTER HUMMED quietly and Louisiana stared at the figures from the November profit-and-loss statement on the screen. New operations had gone in and others had closed down. The price of oil per barrel was holding steady, but with the OPEC meeting scheduled for December, all that could change.

She really didn't care. She wished she did, but she couldn't seem to work up any enthusiasm for it. Since she'd been back, she'd been giving more and more responsibilities to Mrs. Kruger. The woman had handled everything beautifully while Louisiana was in Thailand. She knew the operation backward and forward. Billy Boone Bond never believed in having an uninformed employee, and his secretary was no exception.

Louisiana sat back in her chair and stared out the window at the flat expanse that was her empire. It seemed to spread out forever, with barely a dip or rise in the terrain. Brown and flat. As bland as beans without salt pork.

She closed her eyes and thought of what it had felt like standing that day on Gunner's veranda. There were so many sights and sounds and smells that came back to her now, she didn't know which was the more powerful and intoxicating. Like partaking of a sensual feast, she smelled jasmine and orchids and chicken being roasted by a sidewalk vendor. There was the fetid stench of stagnant *klongs,* the pungent smell of incense smoke rising in a spiral from a tiny shrine. In her mind, the sun dazzled as it struck the golden spires of the temples; it rested easy on the eyes in the shade of a palm. She thought of the heat and the unceasing rain, of wet rice fields and tree-dwelling spirits.

She opened her eyes to the flat baked earth outside the window and wished fervently that it would rain. She tried not to wish for things she couldn't have—like the wish to be standing on Gunner's garden veranda, or to be floating lazily down the River of Kings lying in his arms.

Her daddy had taught her long ago—when, as a child, she had longed for a mother—that it didn't do any good to wish for things you couldn't have. *Daughter,* he would have said to her now, *you hump up and take it like an old bull in a blue norther*.

She glanced once again at the screen full of figures, but it couldn't hold her attention. She reached into the stack of mail and pulled out the latest *Adventures in*

Warfare that Ham had sent. She had already read the message from him and it couldn't have been more clear. He was closing down the publishing office facade and this was his last issue. He was going to spend full-time under Po's teachings. He had helped Roxy get a job in a school and had bought her a small house near some of her relatives.

Louisiana flipped through the pages of the magazine, thinking about Ham and the life he had ahead of him. He had made a choice, at least, something she had not been strong enough to do.

She flipped another page and started reading an article about new camouflage wear.

"I know—you read those magazines for their insightful articles, right?"

Louisiana's head snapped up at the sound of that voice. Her heart began to hammer in her chest. She lost the ability to breathe. Staring at the man standing in the doorway to her office, she repeated to herself, *Don't wish for things that aren't there.*

But he was there, in the flesh, standing in this very doorway wearing cowboy boots with silver spurs, a gun belt and pistol attached at the waist and a black felt Stetson.

He grinned at her and a smile broke out on her face. "No, I like the pictures of all the men," she said. Laughing breathlessly, she added, "You . . . you make quite a picture there yourself, darlin'."

He looked down at his outfit. "What? Too much?"

She stood, hoping her knees wouldn't give way as she walked toward him. He looked great. Her circle of vision was filled with him. He stepped fully into the room as she reached him and he closed the door. They stood facing each other, less than a foot apart, for a long moment, and she drank him in as if she had been lost in a desert for weeks. She wanted to touch him, but her hands felt plastered to her sides.

"What are you doing here?"

"I was on my way back to Bangkok from Washington." He shrugged. "I got lost. Where the hell am I, anyway?"

She smiled. "You're in my little corner of the world now."

His eyes moved to the window beside her desk. "Doesn't look so little to me."

She followed his line of vision. "Sometimes open spaces can be confining."

He looked back at her, surprised, but he held in the words he really wanted to say and the ones she really wanted to hear. "So this is where you do all your wheelin' and dealin', huh?"

Her nerves were shot, so she walked to her desk and sat on one edge, hoping she wasn't going to lose control and say something really stupid. "This is it."

"Well, tell me, what's it like running one of the biggest oil companies in America?"

She sighed. "Crazy. Chaotic. Calamitous."

"So why do you do it?"

Her expression was incredulous. "Because I'm responsible for it."

"Who says?"

"I inherited it, Gunner. Ham wasn't around and . . . and wasn't interested. Daddy Bond raised me to run the company. It was just—I don't know—always expected of me."

"Maybe he expected too much of you."

Her chin lifted in that indignant way of hers. "What is that supposed to mean? I do a damn good job of running Bond Enterprises."

He grinned. "Come on down off your high horse, Louisiana. That's not what I meant. I meant, have you ever thought about what *you* wanted? What *you* expect out of life?"

She sighed again and glanced out the window. "I never got into all that—you know—that me-generation-yuppie stuff. BMWs, primal scream and what have you. It just never was me. I drive a '75 Ford pickup with an embarrassing exhaust problem. I live pretty much the way Billy Boone lived. He wasn't a flashy sort. He didn't believe in a lot of self-analysis. He just did what he damn well wanted to do."

Gunner ambled over to the wall of shelves, his spurs jingling as he walked. He took down a framed photograph of Billy Boone Bond with his two children. Louisiana was ten years old in the picture. He smiled at the photograph, then set it back on the shelf.

He walked over to where she sat and he laid his hands down on the desk on each side of her. His face was very close. "So—you're doing just what you damn well want to do, then." His voice lowered. "You're real happy alone like this . . . without me."

No! she almost blurted out. *It's awful and lonely and miserable without you!* "I get along."

"Get along," he repeated.

"Yes," she whispered.

He flicked off his hat. His gaze dropped from her eyes to her mouth and there it lingered. Her heart felt as if it were going to bump right out of her chest and her throat clamped shut.

"Life doesn't always have to stay the same, Louisiana. Things change. You don't have to be afraid of that."

"Gunner," she whispered softly.

"I can't let you go," he said. "I've tried, but—" he shook his head "—it just hasn't worked. I miss...everything. All those hons and darlin's dropping from your mouth. Even the fact that I can't make you mind."

"You've got Bruno to boss around."

He shook his head. "Nope. Not anymore. He and Savika—you remember the woman you rescued? Well, she and Bruno have sort of set up housekeeping. Now she gets to boss him around instead."

Her hands came up to the sides of his jaw and she grinned. "So I'm supposed to be a substitute for Bruno, is that it?"

His eyes centered on her mouth. "Sort of...but not exactly."

Her fingers slipped into his hair and she pulled him closer. "Then maybe you'd better explain it to me a little better."

His mouth came down over hers, hungrily, feverishly. His hands grasped the sides of her head, holding her captive. Her arms looped around his neck. Outside the window, a hawk circled lazily above the house while black oil rigs pumped up and down in their ceaseless pursuit of deposits laid down aeons ago.

The phone rang, but Louisiana immediately reached over and silenced it. She smiled at Gunner, then punched the button on the intercom. "Mrs. Kruger, could you make sure I'm not disturbed for a while?"

She turned back to Gunner. "We don't want Mrs. Kruger to catch you without your boots on."

Her hands lifted to the gun belt at his waist and slowly released the catch.

THE SUN HOVERED on the western brink, giving one last fiery display before it melted into the horizon. Gunner sat in the leather swivel chair at her desk, his bare feet on the desk. Louisiana sat on top of the desk, her feet in his lap.

"So what are we going to do about this?" he asked quietly, massaging her toes between his fingers. "I can't fly back over here every time I have the uncontrollable urge to propose to you."

Louisiana's eyes locked with his for a long moment. Finally she stood. "Excuse me for just a sec, sugar." She grinned at him and walked out of the office, coming back a minute later with the secretary.

Louisiana led Mrs. Kruger into the office. Gunner dropped his feet to the floor and stood, moving to the side of the desk.

"Is there something you need?" asked Mrs. Kruger.

"Yes, there is. I need you to sit in this chair." She led her to the desk and sat her in the swivel desk chair. "Now how does that feel?" Louisiana asked.

"I beg your pardon?"

Louisiana sat on the edge of the desk and folded her arms over her waist. "I think you fit real good there, Mrs. Kruger."

"But—but this is your desk! Why am I sitting at your desk?"

"Well," she said slowly, "because I am going on an extended vacation." She glanced up at Gunner. He was leaning against the wall, smiling at her. She wondered how she had ever survived this last month and a half without him. "I'm going to be in Thailand for a while."

"Thailand! What on earth for!" Her startled gaze jumped back and forth from Louisiana to Gunner. "Ah," she finally said with an expression of polite noncommitment. "You, er, you intend to peruse the opportunities there for corporate expansion."

Louisiana grinned. "Very good. I like that." She looked at Gunner. "Don't you like that, hon?"

"Like it a lot."

Louisiana stood. "That is exactly what I am going to do, Mrs. Kruger. I am going to peruse the opportunities there for corporate expansion." She walked over to Gunner and took his arm. They headed for the door. "Oh, and by the way," she said, turning around to face the still-dazed woman. "I might just land myself a husband while I'm at it."

Mrs. Kruger stared at the doorway through which they walked. She sat very rigid and straight for a long time, trying to make sense of this odd turn of events. Things had always been odd around the Bond household, but this . . .

After several stiff minutes, she allowed her shoulders to relax. But only a little.

Several minutes later, she leaned back in the chair. And very, very slowly, she lifted one leg and then the other until her no-nonsense black patent shoes were resting on the top of the desk.

She glanced out the window at the black rigs pumping against a coral sky. She looked at the profit-and-loss statement still frozen on the computer screen.

She picked up the soldier-of-fortune magazine and tossed it in the trash, then she pulled the keyboard into her lap and began the long process of analyzing the financial data on the screen. Her attention wavered and her gaze drifted down to the trash can. She reached in and pulled out the magazine, then propped it up on the desk.

The robust soldier on the cover of *Adventures in Warfare* was looking directly at her.

HARLEQUIN®

Temptation®

the **Fortune Boys**

A funny, sexy miniseries from bestselling
author Elise Title!

**LOSING THEIR HEARTS MEANT
LOSING THEIR FORTUNES....**

If any of the four Fortune brothers were unfortunate enough to
wed, they'd be permanently divorced from the Fortune
millions—thanks to their father's last will and testament.

BUT CUPID HAD OTHER PLANS!
Meet Adam in #412 **ADAM & EVE** (Sept. 1992)
Meet Peter #416 **FOR THE LOVE OF PETE**
(Oct. 1992)
Meet Truman in #420 **TRUE LOVE** (Nov. 1992)
Meet Taylor in #424 **TAYLOR MADE** (Dec. 1992)

**WATCH THESE FOUR MEN TRY TO WIN
AT LOVE AND NOT FORFEIT $$$**

HE CROSSED TIME FOR HER

Captain Richard Colter rode the high seas, brandished a
sword and pillaged treasure ships. A swashbuckling
privateer, he was a man with voracious appetites and a lust
for living. And in the eighteenth century, any woman
swooned at his feet for the favor of his wild passion. History
had it that Captain Richard Colter went down with his ship,
the *Black Cutter,* in a dazzling sea battle off the Florida
coast in 1792.

Then what was he doing washed ashore on a Key West
beach in 1992—alive?

MARGARET ST. GEORGE brings you an extraspecial love
story this month, about an extraordinary man who would
do anything for the woman he loved:

#462 THE PIRATE AND HIS LADY
by Margaret St. George

*When love is meant to be, nothing can stand in its
way . . . not even time.*

Don't miss American Romance
#462 THE PIRATE AND HIS LADY.
It's a love story you'll never forget.